Website: elaineguginmaddex.com

Bookstores and wholesale orders can be made through
Red Tuque Books Inc. at www.redtuquebooks.ca
Cover art design: Magdalene Carson

Library and Archives Canada Cataloguing in Publication

Maddex, Elaine Gugin, 1955-, author
Wise woman's manor / Elaine Gugin Maddex.

Issued in print and electronic formats.
ISBN 978-1-987982-11-4 (paperback).--ISBN 978-1-987982-12-1 (pdf)

I. Title.

PS8626.A3144W57 2016   C813'.6   C2016-900081-8
                                            C2016-900082-6

Artistic Warrior
www.artisticwarrior.com

DISCLAIMER

Wise Woman's Manor

Elaine Gugin Maddex

An Artistic Warrior Publication

To those who watch over us from above.
For me it's our sweet angel Piper, my dear
brother Jim, my parents and all those before.

Granny Gugin, I especially feel you in the
garden and when I put pen to paper.
Thank you for your guidance!

Contents

RECIPES

Hope you enjoy !! :)
EMaddex

1
The Turning of a Difficult Guest

The newly engaged Tessy McGuigan lay snuggled in her bed, admiring her stunning Celtic antique emerald and diamond ring under the glow of her bedside lamp. The Christmas presents had all been opened and in the last few days the turkey leftovers had been turned into bunwiches, casseroles, soups and stews. Aye, life at Ashling Manor had eased back into a more manageable pace.

Tessy threw off her thick quilt and rolled out of bed. Being December 28th in Ladyslipper, Saskatchewan, it was still very dark and very cold. She wriggled her toes into her plush slippers, pulled on her cozy, long terry housecoat and headed to the kitchen to let out her dogs, Duke and Darby, and to feed her cats, Merlin and Cordelia. She had just reached the bottom landing when the dogs started barking. "Who in St. Paddy's name would be at my door this time of the mornin'?" she wondered out loud. She opened it to find her betrothed, Marshall Tayse, standing in the cold. He grumbled something about "that wretched woman" and brushed past her. He stopped his griping long enough to lean down and give Tessy a peck on the cheek.

"Morning," he growled.

"Good mornin', dear," Tessy calmly replied as she closed the door. "What is it that's got ye all in a flap so early in the day, love?"

"Oh, that, that, that woman – or should I say tyrant – has got everyone in a flap!" he complained as he waved his arms wildly in the air.

Tessy turned to hide a smirk. She knew Marshall was talking about Grandma Tucker, his son-in-law's mother who had come from

British Columbia for a visit over the Christmas holidays. Marshall was staying with his daughter Penny, son-in-law Jim, and their three children: Sarah, soon to be 16; Matt, 13; and Emma, seven. However, he was not enjoying his visit as much as usual. Tessy had been invited over to the Tuckers' earlier in the week to have the pleasure of meeting Grandma Tucker. She'd soon discovered that she was what a person might describe as somewhat difficult.

"That woman can clear a room quicker than a skunk!" Marshall continued, following Tessy down the hall to the kitchen. Tessy decided a large pot of strong coffee might suit this morning a mite better than tea. She let the dogs out, fed the cats and got the coffee brewing.

"Penny is beside herself trying to please her and it just can't be done! She won't lift a finger to help with anything, and she expects to be waited on hand and foot. She doesn't even listen to her own son. She can't figure out why anyone in their right mind would move to a place like Ladyslipper, let alone drag along their family and start a business. And, I have never known the kids to hide out in their rooms as much as they have in the last few days... even little Emma!" he huffed as he plunked himself down at the kitchen table.

Tessy turned again, to hide a flat out giggle this time, and got caught.

"And what is so funny, my bride-to-be?" Marshall finally smiled at her, realizing his disgruntled mood was perhaps a bit dramatic. He pulled her onto his lap and gave her a real kiss. "Good morning, sweetheart. I'm sorry. We haven't even been engaged a full week and here I am already sounding like a grumpy old man. But that woman could turn a saint miserable!" he started up again.

Tessy hugged his neck and laughed heartily. "Well now, perhaps I may have to pay another visit to Grandma Tucker. Sounds like she just needs a little sprinkling of change of perspective."

"Won't do any good. She's impossible to reason with!" Marshall blurted.

"Aye, maybe. But leave it to me, dear. Would ye like a cup of coffee, Dr. Tayse? And possibly a bite of breakfast might settle ye down a mite?" And with that, Tessy hopped off his lap and began to scurry around the kitchen.

An hour later, Marshall was well fed, coffeed out, and much calmer. "So… when are you coming to visit me in Winnipeg?" he asked as he got up to help clear the dishes.

"Well love, I would like to say soon, but since I've started my natural healing department at Jim's pharmacy we've been so busy I'm not sure when I will be able to get away. Things might slow down in January. Did I tell ye I've named it The Wee Nook of Herbals and Oils?"

Marshall laughed. "I love it. Only you could come up with the perfect name. Good for you. But getting back to my original question, we do have a wedding to plan, my lady. And it will never be too soon for me. I promise not to turn into a grumpy old man, well… as long as that woman keeps her distance from me. Speaking of which, I suppose I should stop hiding out and head back to give Penny and the kids some support."

"All right, love. I'll pop over this afternoon." She glanced into the air and slowly added, "I have something special I want to prepare first."

"Okay, but don't be long. You are our last hope of any happiness for the remainder of the week."

Tessy laughed, reached for his hand, pulled the reluctant guest to the foyer, and sent him back out into the cold December morning. She closed the door and leaned up against it. She stared into the distance and tapped her bottom lip with her finger.

"Now," she mused aloud, "now, for Grandma Tucker," and headed to her herbal kitchen. Tessy's herbal kitchen is situated at the back of the main kitchen and is where Tessy concocts all her herbal lotions, potions and remedies. Some she makes for specific means only, especially when all else fails. This appeared to be one of those occasions. As she mixed the ingredients with great care, love and intent she chanted:

Makin' tea and cookies filled with love.
Ingredients from Mother Earth and intensions from above.
Heavenly aroma and tasty as can be
Let everyone that samples them be filled with glee.
This is my will – so mote it be.

As Grandma Tucker had everyone on a very strict, precise schedule, which was gladly adhered to in order to keep an amicable environment, Tessy arrived at 2 p.m. sharp, just in time for afternoon tea. She did not, however, arrive empty handed. She brought two tins with her. One contained an herbal tea blend and the other was filled with fresh-baked cookies. She also brought a lovely new journal and pen.

Now, Grandma Tucker only drank one type of tea, which Penny had to hunt long and hard for before her arrival, so it took a great deal of persuasion to get her to agree to try Tessy's mix.

"Oh, all right then!" she barked. "But only because I am a gracious person and don't want to be any trouble. But if it tastes like dishwater I'm not drinking it!"

Penny sighed and threw Tessy a glance while she spooned the mix into the teapot. Tessy smirked and patted Penny's hand. Penny thanked Tessy as she popped the lid off the tin of cookies and started placing them on a small decorative platter.

"What are those?" Grandma Tucker demanded. "They smell good enough, but they look like small cow patties."

Penny placed her hand over her bowed face and shook her head.

Tessy laughed. "Aye, I suppose they do. They are made with oats, seeds, some whole wheat, and dried fruit with a few herbs and spices, is all. They are quite delicious and I made them, 'specially, for you. Please give one a try," coaxed Tessy.

"I will, but I'd better not be sitting on the toilet for the rest of the day!" Grandma Tucker warned. Penny was horrified at the comment but again, Tessy just laughed.

While Penny finished making the tea and setting the table, Tessy sat down next to Grandma and pulled the journal and pen out of her bag. "Mrs. Tucker, I brought you a little something."

"Thank you, but what I am suppose to do with this?" she questioned as she gingerly inspected it.

"Well, I find that if I write down my thoughts and aspirations, especially at the beginning of a new year, things just seem to appear a little clearer and fall into place."

"Well, I'm pretty sure that's not going to happen. I could perhaps use it for recipes, though," she said as she set the journal to the side and reached for a cookie.

None of the kids made an appearance and Jim and Marshall were hiding down at the pharmacy putting up some new shelving so it was just Penny, Tessy and Grandma Tucker enjoying afternoon tea. Surprisingly enough, Grandma had two cups of tea with a cookie for each. Tessy shared the story of how she and Marshall had met and the night of their first date when Marshall had taken an unfortunate tumble over her back step. Grandma Tucker started to laugh. Penny was stunned! She couldn't believe her eyes nor could she remember the last time she had heard her mother-in-law honestly laugh.

"Well, Tessy, that must have been quite a shock for you both?" Grandma Tucker smiled. "You are so lucky to have found love late in life. I lost my James eleven years ago and it's too late for me now. I am just living out my days one at time, one much like the other."

"My good Mrs. Tucker. That's the whole point! It's not late in life. As they say, 'tis the first day of the rest of your life, so go and live it to the fullest. It's not too late for ye to get out there, have some fun, and possibly meet a charming gentleman. Look at what happened to me. When I least expected it, there stood Dr. Marshall Tayse! And here I am 'bout to be a bride all over again."

"You know, Tessy, and please call me Eileen, I might just give that a try. They keep asking me to join the seniors' group down at the Centre back home. I just assumed it was a bunch of old people playing checkers, but I hear they have interesting outings, dances once a week, and even Hawaiian Hula lessons on Thursday evenings."

"That sounds like grand fun, Eileen. Who knows, there could even be a chance of some magical outcomes." Tessy winked as she smiled and patted her hand.

"Well, if you'll excuse me, I think I'll go up to my room and jot down a few things in this lovely journal you brought for me. Thank you, Tessy, for the journal and for our wonderful visit this afternoon. Penny dear, please call me when you are ready to start supper. I would like to help. Bye-bye now."

Flabbergasted, Penny absently answered, "Y-y-yes. Certainly. Thank you, Eileen."

Tessy got up to leave as well. Penny walked her to the door. "Tessy, is what happened, what I think just happened?"

"Whatever do you mean, Penny dear?" Tessy replied, not turning as she spoke.

"Well, I have no idea what you put in that tea or those cookies, but thank you from the bottom of my heart," Penny continued with amusement in her voice and eyebrows raised.

"The first two ingredients I put in anything I prepare are love and intent, my dear… love and intent. That, and nudging one's attention to a new outlook, never hurts," she added, reaching for a hug. She gave Penny a smile and a wink and walked out the door.

The remainder of Grandma Tucker's visit was noticeably much more pleasant.

2
A Fresh Outlook and Misconceptions

New Year's Eve morning, Tessy took her breakfast tea into the library to have a little chat with her late husband, Dermot. Tessy knows that Dermot is never far from her and that it was he who initiated things between her and Marshall. His presence is always most vivid in the library, so when she needs to be with him that is where she goes.

"Good mornin' darlin'. Well, here we are at the end of another blessed year. And what a blessed year it has been! I don't even know where to begin to thank ye for all ye've done for me. All your scalawaggin' around until ye finally made it clear as to what it was ye were up to. Aye, ye've picked a fine man for me – very much like you, yet very different. But remember, I'm still expecting ye to be here come rain or shine. There'll be things I can only talk to ye about. Things that only you will understand." She stroked the top of the large, dark mahogany desk where Dermot once sat for hours at a time. She finished her tea while reminiscing cherished memories of their time together.

Over at the Tuckers, the morning was not quite so serene. Everyone was scurrying around getting Grandma Tucker ready for her flight home. Penny was in the kitchen preparing a hearty breakfast, Jim and Marshall were hauling suitcases out to the car, and the children were spending some actual quality time with Grandma.

Jim was putting the last of the load in the car when Tessy pulled up. "Good morning," Jim greeted her.

"Good mornin' to ye, Jim. Looks like Eileen is packed and ready to go, then," Tessy replied.

"Yep. Guess that's it for this visit. Tessy, I want to thank you for smoothing things over for us and helping my mother see life with a bit better outlook."

"Well, Jim, I really didn't do anything. All we did was have a nice afternoon tea and chat."

"I have a feeling it was a little something more than that." Jim smiled at her.

Tessy remained silent and followed Jim into the house. Marshall walked past the door just as Tessy entered. He immediately gathered her up in his arms. "Tessy! Good morning. What a nice surprise. What are you doing here?"

"Mornin' love," she said. "I've just popped in to say my farewells to Eileen."

The kids ran to see who was at the door. "Tessy!" Emma called out as she flung herself around Tessy's midsection.

"Good mornin', my wee darling," Tessy hugged her back.

"Grandma is leaving today," Emma informed her.

"Aye, darling. I heard that she was. I bet you're going to miss her."

"Yeah, I am now. Not before, but I am now," was her honest reply.

Jim quickly glanced around to make sure his mother was out of ear shot which, thankfully, she was. "Emma, I would like you to go wash up before breakfast, please." He smiled at Tessy. "Will you join us for breakfast, Tessy?"

"Oh, no. I wouldn't want to intrude," Tessy replied.

"Not at all. Please. Penny and Mother would love the visit," Jim insisted.

"And me too," Marshall smiled, pulling her close.

"And me too," Sarah agreed. "Besides, if you have a minute after breakfast, Cherokee is coming over and we have some questions about the healing kits you gave us for Christmas."

"Of course, dear. All right, then, that would be lovely. Thank ye. I'll head into the kitchen to see if Penny needs a hand. I'm assuming that's where I'll find Eileen, as well."

Soon everyone was seated at the table for a full breakfast fit for the cold morning it was, and enjoying some light conversation.

"Well Mother, your visit just didn't seem long enough. I sure wish you'd consider staying another week," Jim earnestly suggested.

"Thank you, son. I've had a wonderful time, but I'm actually looking forward to getting home and starting my new year with a fresh outlook and… " she glanced up at him and raised her eyebrows, "possibly an unexpected adventure or two."

Everyone laughed.

"Ooooooh, Grandma! You go girl! Sarah reached over and gave her Grandma a high five.

"Good for you, Eileen," Tessy added. "I believe this is going to be a year of adventure for us all. I feel it in me bones."

"Sounds intriguing, my lady. I'm looking forward to finding out what that means," Marshall said, eyes twinkling.

"Well Mother, if we don't want that adventure to start off on the wrong foot we had better get you to the airport on time. It's about an hour's drive, so you and I should be heading off pretty soon in order to have you there in time for check in."

With everyone bustling around looking for any items Grandma may have missed, Tessy was able to pull her aside for a moment. "Eileen dear, it was such a pleasure to meet ye and for us to spend some time getting to know one another. Here is my mailing address and telephone number should ye want to be in touch. I would really enjoy hearing from you from time to time. Here is a tin of that nice tea we had the other day and I mixed up a little bottle of homemade perfume just for you. I suggest ye dab just a bit behind your ears and some on the inside of your wrists before ye go off to one of those dances. It could very possibly help make that adventure appear even sooner than we expect." Tessy leaned in close to her and winked.

"Why, Tessy McGuigan! I'm beginning to understand some of what I have heard about you. Thank you. I feel one's life is much better for befriending you. I think we shall stay in touch."

The two new friends hugged and said their good-byes.

It wasn't long before they had Grandma Tucker buckled in to the SUV, and she and Jim were on their way to the airport. Just as they got to the end of the block, they noticed Sarah's best friend, Cherokee, making her way to the house. She waved good-bye to them. When she arrived, she knocked and let herself in. She found everyone in the kitchen cleaning up.

"Morning, everyone," she chirped as she picked up a tea towel and grabbed a pan to dry.

"Morning, sweetheart," Penny smiled. "You don't have to dry dishes."

"Well, you know what Tessy says, many hands make light work." she replied, throwing Tessy a big smile.

"Aye. Very true, my dear, very true," Tessy said as she lovingly patted her on the back.

With the kitchen clean and Penny knowing the girls wanted to discuss some things with Tessy, she excused herself and asked Emma to help her clean the guest room. Matthew and Grandpa were on their way down to the rink for hockey practice.

The girls soon had Tessy's full attention. "Now girls, what is it that ye need to ask me?"

Cherokee began. "Well, Tessy… we've been going through the books you included with our kits and we can't find any spells in them."

Tessy started to laugh. The girls looked surprised. "Oh, I'm sorry, girls. I'm not laughing at you. It's just that so many people just assume that if ye work with herbs, oils and gemstones that you are automatically associated with the Craft."

"But all the things that you've done… just look at how you fixed Grandma Tucker. That HAD to be magick!" Sarah piped.

Again, Tessy laughed. "Oh, sweetheart. Aye, I may have said a wee chant while I was preparing my gift, but it is the love and intent behind the ingredients that made the magick. All I did was sit with your grandmother, had a lovely chat, and she ended up with the realization, on her own, that there might be a different, more pleasant outcome to her future."

"But can't you just put a spell on someone?" Sarah asked.

"Ye may change the energy in the room, but ye must never manipulate nor tamper with another person's free will. It must, first and foremost, be for the good of all. Harm none, do what ye will. I am so sorry if I have given ye any misconceptions about the world of spiritual and natural healing. I'm thinking the sooner we get started on our lessons the better, before any more misunderstandings pop up."

3
Out with the Old... In with the New

On New Year's Eve in Ladyslipper, there are several choices as to how to celebrate it. There is a dinner and dance at the Community Hall for adults only, or for family fun there is a hayride, skating, a bonfire, food booths and fireworks at the park in the center of town. Since this was the Tuckers' first New Year's Eve in Ladyslipper, they decided to spend it as a family. And, of course, having Grandpa Tayse staying with them made it even more special. The park festivities started at 7 p.m., so about 6 p.m. everyone began to get ready, making sure there were enough dry, warm mitts, tuques and scarves for all. Marshall announced he was going over to pick up Tessy and would be back shortly.

Marshall arrived to find Tessy already bundled up, skates in hand and eager to get going. She was so looking forward to this New Year's Eve. For the last few years she had spent it by herself, reflecting on the year just ending and anticipating the unknown of the one to come. She had never minded spending it in solitude for she enjoyed her own company. But this year, this year was something to be celebrated and what better way to ring it in than with her soon-to-be new family.

When Tessy flung open the door with such exuberance, Marshall had to laugh at her childlike enthusiasm. *Oh, how I love this woman!* he thought.

"Well, it's a grand thing to see ye standing at my door in much better humour than the last," Tessy greeted him.

He gathered her up in his arms and kissed her earnestly. "Let's go enjoy our first New Year's Eve together, sweetheart."

"I thought ye'd never ask," Tessy teased. Then hand in hand they ran down the steps and jumped in the car.

When they entered the Tuckers' foyer, everyone was ready to go except for little Emma.

"What happened?" Grandpa asked. "When I left you were standing at the door fully dressed and chomping at the bit to get going."

"I wasn't chomping on anything, Grandpa," Emma looked puzzled.

Everyone laughed.

"Oh, at the last minute she had to go to the bathroom so everything had to come off – her coat, scarf, boots, snow pants – well, Dad, you know the routine. There's not a parent alive that doesn't know the routine," Penny said, shaking her head.

Tessy chuckled as Grandpa helped Emma get her boots and mitts back on.

It was going to be extremely busy downtown and as it was such a beautiful evening – cold, but with no wind – they decided to leave the car at home and walk. Jim plunked Emma on the toboggan along with the extra blankets and a backpack full of any possible requirements and they all took turns pulling her. Through the crisp, still air they could hear festive music resonating from the church's tall steeple speakers. They could see a soft glow in the distance from the Christmas lights and the flickering of the huge bonfire reflecting off the night sky. Their quickened pace became apparent, matching their eagerness to join in the fun. The closer they got to the action, they met more and more friends, neighbours and co-workers all exchanging welcoming salutations of excitement and anticipation. Sarah spotted Cherokee and ran over to her, while Matt met up with his best buds, Brendon and Jason, and off they all went to join the rest of their chums at the large outdoor skating rink. Emma hopped off the toboggan and was wildly looking around for her very best friend, Becky.

"Mommy, I don't see her anywhere. She promised she and her mommy would be here," Emma cried.

"Relax, honey. She'll be here somewhere," reassured her mother. "Let's go over to where the hayrides are and take a look. You know how much Becky loves horses. They'll probably be over there."

Marshall took Tessy's hand. "Well, my lady. Do you think you are limber enough to put on the old skates and go for a spin around the rink?"

"Really! Limber enough, ye say? Well, I don't know 'bout you, but I am ready and raring to go and I'll be skating circles around ye before ye even get your balance."

"Ooooh, you're on, my sweet lady!" And they raced off with their skates to find the nearest unoccupied bench, leaving Jim standing all alone tending the toboggan and watching the last of his family disappear.

"That didn't take long! Scattered like mice," he said, glancing around and shaking his head.

Emma found Becky petting one of the horses with her mommy standing nearby talking to one of the other moms. As soon as Emma spotted her she yelled "Becky!" and ran over to her friend. The two little girls, not having seen one another for more than a week, hugged and rocked back and forth. Susan, Becky's mother, smiled and said to Penny, "Do you think they missed one another?"

Penny laughed, "You'd think. How was your Christmas?"

"Fine, thanks. We were in Moose Jaw. It was my ex's turn to have Becky for Christmas day, but my sister and her family live there as well so we celebrated a day early with them. It all worked out just fine."

"That's wonderful. It's so nice to celebrate it with family, and how lucky to have them in Moose Jaw, as well. Have you heard about the exciting news happening in our household?"

"Yes! That is such exciting news! Where are the newly engaged couple? I can't wait to congratulate them."

"Mommy, can we go on the hayride now? Please!" begged Becky, tugging at her mother's arm.

"Yeah, can we Mommy?" Emma joined in.

"Yes, of course, dear," Penny assured. "But just let me go find your father first. I'm sure he's probably looking for us."

"Penny, if you want to go ahead and find Jim, I will take the girls on the hayride and you can catch up with us later," offered Susan.

"Oh, Susan, thank you. Are you sure you don't mind?"

"Not at all. We'll see you in a bit."

Penny trundled off, turning in time to see the girls being lifted on to the wagon. Dodging as many people as she could, she finally spotted Jim standing over by the edge of the rink watching the kids and chatting with a fellow proprietor. Penny snuck up behind Jim and hooked her arm inside his as she said her hellos. They all exchanged small talk for a few more moments, then excused themselves.

"Where are the girls?" Jim asked looking around and sounding slightly concerned.

"Oh, they're fine. They're with Susan on the hayride."

"Why doesn't that surprise me?" Jim smiled.

"Honey, why don't we go get some hot apple cider to warm up, then come back and watch the kids skate for a while?" suggested Penny.

"Great idea!"

About an hour later, the whole family, plus a couple of extras, were all together and starving. After scouting out the various food booths, their choices were chili, vegetarian lasagna, hot dogs and hamburgers. While Jim and Marshall took the girls' order and went to stand in line, the girls hovered over a group of people looking like they were ready to vacate one of the picnic tables. Matt and his buddies were off getting their burgers, then heading back to the rink. By the time Marshall and Jim returned with the food, the girls were all settled in at the table. "I suggest we eat fairly quickly before everything cools off!" Marshall advised. With all the exercise and fresh air, appetites were hearty so there was little chance of much cooling off. It wasn't long before everyone was fed and ready to be on the move again.

Sarah and Cherokee excused themselves and said they were going over to the bonfire to meet with some of their friends. Emma and Becky begged for another hayride, and the rest of the family decided to join them. As Marshall was helping Tessy up on to the wagon, he flashed back to the first hayride he'd experienced in Ladyslipper. It was at Tessy's Christmas in July party last summer when he first met and instantly fell in love with her. As they snuggled close and deep into the hay under a blanket, they reminisced, laughed and counted their blessings. The large, red wagon glided up and down the snow-covered streets while its passengers sang some old familiar songs and enjoyed the Christmas lights and cheerful decorations.

Once the wagon came to a stop and the group climbed off, the Tuckers decided to get a cup of hot chocolate and go warm up by the bonfire. Tessy and Marshall were standing in line to order when Tessy looked over and noticed her nemesis, Mrs. Chamberlain, sitting in a car watching the festivities.

"Marshall, love, would you please order an extra hot chocolate? I would like to take one over to Mrs. Chamberlain."

"Seriously?" Marshall blurted out.

Tessy chuckled. "Yes, dear."

"After all the terrible things she has said and done to you over the years, you would do that?" Marshall ordered three hot chocolates.

"Aye. We've made a slight breakthrough in our world of differences so I would, hopefully, like to continue on that path. And she did send me that lovely Christmas arrangement. Trust me, I am not expecting miracles, just making an effort."

"Okay. But I think it's a baaaad idea. Here you go, dear. Good luck. I think you're going to need it!" Marshall volunteered as he handed her the cup.

"Thank ye, love," Tessy said as she gave him a peck.

Tessy was having slight misgivings as she made her way over to the vehicle. Mrs. Chamberlain was not, nor likely ever to be, a fan of Tessy McGuigan. Just because Tessy happened to help Mrs. Chamberlain a couple of weeks ago when she fell and hurt her ankle didn't mean anything would change between them. And Tessy was afraid of that. This is the right thing to do, Tessy repeated as she reached her destination.

Mrs. Chamberlain lowered the window and stared at Tessy.

"Good evening, Mrs. Chamberlain. How are you feeling?" Tessy smiled.

"Fine, thank you," was Mrs. Chamberlain's curt response.

"Glad to hear it. I thought ye might like some hot chocolate to warm your bones," Tessy said as she handed the cup to her.

"Thank you, but why would you bring me hot chocolate?" She sounded quite indignant.

"I just thought that since ye were unable to get around on your ankle yet that I would bring you some."

"Don't think that anything has changed between us, Ms. McGuigan. I thank you for your good deed, but I still do not like your ways. And that flower arrangement was my husband's doing, not mine!"

"I didn't come over to convert ye, Mrs. Chamberlain. I just came to give ye a cup of hot chocolate," Tessy sighed.

"You didn't put anything in it, did you?" she asked as she suspiciously sniffed and peered into the cup of dark rich brew.

Tessy dropped her chin and shook her head. "No, Mrs. Chamberlain. It is just plain old hot chocolate. Good night to ye. Happy New Year." And she walked away feeling disheartened. As she approached Marshall he held out her hot chocolate to her, raised his eyebrows, and with a sad expression said, "It didn't go well, did it?" He put his free arm around her.

"Nye, I shouldn't be surprised. I guess ye can't change a leopard's spots. Nor a grizzly's growl!" she added as she grinned up at him.

"Come on, my lady. Let's head on over to the fire and join the others."

The festivities were winding down and the fireworks were set to go off around 10 p.m. When first planning this event, the committee had wanted to have them displayed at midnight, but then they decided midnight would be a bit too late for all the little ones. So 10 p.m. it was.

The crowd was repositioning itself towards the riverbank to get the best viewing point. Jim loaded Emma and Becky on the toboggan while Penny draped a warm blanket around the two sleepyheads. Then they were off to find their spot. They collected the other kids along the way, with Susan, Tessy and Marshall as well. They soon found the perfect spot just across from where the fireworks were to go off.

They were spectacular! They popped and banged with an explosion of brilliant colour while everyone oohed and ahhed with delight. About half an hour later they had the grand finale, and people began breaking off in all directions. The Tuckers were among them.

They hadn't even exited the park's edge when the two little girls were off to dreamland, snuggled close and cozy. The older kids all went ahead home to pop some popcorn and put on a movie. Susan and Becky lived a block over from the Tuckers, so the remaining few went off in that direction. When they reached their home, Jim asked Susan if she would like him to carry Becky into the house.

"Thank you, Jim, but I have to get her out of all those layers of clothes, so she is going to have to be awake long enough for that anyway. Thanks just the same, and for getting us this far." She leaned over and gently shook Becky awake. "Come on, sweetheart. Let's get you into the house and ready for bed. Good night and Happy New Year!" She smiled and gave Penny and Tessy a hug.

"Happy New Year!" the gang chimed back.

They crossed over to the next block and made their way home. Jim carried Emma into the house, and they peeled off her heavy clothes and got her tucked into bed. Penny returned to find Jim, Tessy and Marshall enjoying a nightcap. Jim handed Penny her glass and they all toasted to the upcoming New Year.

"Were you and Penny planning on staying up to ring in the New Year?" Marshall enquired.

"Yep. What do you have in mind?" Jim asked.

"Well, we've got almost an hour. How about we play the horse racing game for a while?" Marshall suggested.

"Great! I'll put the TV on so we don't miss the countdown. Penny, do you know where the game is?"

A few minutes later the game was on and Marshall was calling out "…and they're off!"

Before they knew it the countdown to midnight had begun. United they chimed: "Ten, nine, eight, seven." Marshall drew Tessy close and put his arms around her with those mesmerizing blue eyes smiling down at her. Tessy's heart was so full she thought it was going to burst. *Thank ye, Lord, for giving me this moment and many more to come,* instantly ran through her mind. "Four, three, two, one! Happy New Year!"

Marshall kissed Tessy until she was dizzy and her legs turned to jelly.

It was Jim who finally broke the moment. "Okay, you two. At least give us a chance to wish you all the best."

Everyone laughed.

"Oh, Happy New Year, ye two." Tessy reached for Penny, then Jim for a hug and a kiss.

Marshall grabbed Jim's hand and gave it a hearty shake, then pulled his daughter close for a hug and a kiss. "Happy New Year! I know it's going to be the best year of all for me," he added as he gazed at Tessy.

All of a sudden the kids thundered upstairs from the rec room to wish everyone a Happy New Year. Soon the living room was a hub of activity. Once all the hugs and best wishes had been exchanged, everyone said their good nights. Matt and Brendon went back downstairs to finish the movie and bed down there for the night. Sarah and Cherokee headed upstairs to Sarah's bedroom to giggle and chat until they would fall asleep. Marshall went out to warm up the car to take Tessy home. Jim pulled Tessy's coat out of the front closet and helped her on with it.

"Thank ye, Jim. And thank ye both for a most wonderful New Years. What an enjoyable evening of fun and frolic. Sorry it must come to an end," Tessy sighed with pleasure and exhaustion.

Marshall returned rubbing his hands together and blowing on them. "I think we better wait a minute or two for the old girl to warm up."

They remained in the foyer talking about the evening and waiting for the car to heat. After a few minutes, Marshall opened the front door for Tessy and as she started out he leaned in close to Jim and whispered, "Don't wait up for me." He flashed a mischievous smile and winked. Tessy was wondering what struck Jim so funny as Marshall helped her down the steps and into the car.

When the arrived at Tessy's door they stomped the snow off their boots. Tessy asked if Marshall would like to come in for a while.

"Actually, my love, I was wanting to ask you a very important question," Marshall sheepishly asked as he removed his jacket and scarf.

"Aye, and what would that be?" Tessy gingerly asked.

"If we could go upstairs so I could show you just how much I love you." He took her hand and kissed it.

Tessy blushed like a schoolgirl. "What about the children?"

"I'd be home before they get up," Marshall raised his eyebrows.

"Oh, Marshall. I want to show ye how much I love you, too, and I thought I was ready, but now I just don't know if I really am," was her honest reply.

"I don't want to rush you if you're not sure. It has to be right for both of us."

"I appreciate that, love. I knew this was coming about, and my anticipation has been increasing. I really have been looking forward to being intimate with you."

"Okay, please stop saying stuff like that! You have already been driving me crazy without any of that kind of talk."

Tessy laughed and wrapped her arms around him. They started kissing, and before they knew it they were heading upstairs and fell into Tessy's big plush bed.

It was 6 a.m. when Marshall quietly snuck into the Tuckers' foyer.

4
The Afterglow and the Aftermath

Tessy lay snuggled down deep under her comforter, basking in the afterglow that can only occur when one is truly in love and has just physically experienced it.

She had kissed Marshall goodbye and now she was giggling like a school girl. *Aye, ye've still got it, lass! It's been a very long time since I've sampled that kind of passion. I guess some things do improve with time and a little know-how!* She rolled over and fell back into a gleeful, relaxed sleep.

About an hour and a half later she awoke feeling euphoric and very grateful. A little toot escaped from under the blankets.

"Whoop-tuddy!" she winced. "Oh my, I'm sure glad he wasn't here to witness that. However, I suppose I am of the age where it is bound to happen more often." She giggled as she remembered, as a wee girl over in Ireland, her Granny using that term whenever she passed wind. Tessy had learned, at a very early age, to step away when she heard a "whoop-tuddy." Oh my… then there's the wee problem of what Dermot called my "purring like a panther." The things one had to consider when one was thinking of cohabitating. Before long, her thoughts changed and she started to retrace the beautiful images of last evening. She smiled, softly sighed, and climbed out of bed. She shook herself back into reality, gave herself a quick grounding, reached for her housecoat, and wiggled into her slippers. The dogs were waiting, not so patiently, to be let out.

"Good mornin' to ye," she said as she gave them each a good pet before she opened the door. She turned on the back porch light so she could watch them race through the snow, playing, before she went back into the kitchen. She felt she should go into the library and explain things to Dermot, but she wasn't quite sure where to begin. She supposed he already knew and, in fact, probably had his hand in it. How does one explain, to one's deceased husband, about an evening of ecstasy with another man? She decided she would need a little time and a strong cup of coffee before tackling this delicate situation.

She sat at the table for three cups of coffee, which she didn't really want, and was no closer to feeling any clarification on the subject. "I could use a little help here, Dermot," she said out loud. Just then the phone rang. Still deep in thought, she answered.

"Good mornin' to ye!" she greeted.

"The best morning ever, my darling," was the soft, sexy answer she received.

"Aye, I would agree," Tessy bashfully replied as her cheeks turned pink.

"Did you get any sleep after I left, sweetheart?" Marshall asked, truly concerned.

"Aye, I did nod off for a bit. Ye don't let a girl get much beauty sleep, Dr. Tayse." Tessy teased.

"There are some girls that just don't need any," Marshall quipped.

Tessy laughed. "You are a charmer, if little else, Marshall Tayse."

"Since I only have a couple of days left here I want… no… need to see you as much as possible. We really should, at least, start discussing some wedding arrangements. But first and foremost, I was wondering if you could come over later this morning. I am going to Skype all my kids and I really want you to meet them, and them you. They're in all parts of the world so we had to pick a time that might work best for us all. And that time is 11 o'clock this morning."

"Of course, love. I've been waiting to meet the rest of your fine family. Oh my… what should I wear?" She was actually talking more to herself. "Aye, I best wear blue," she continued.

"Anything would look lovely on you, dear. But why blue?" Marshall wasn't sure he should have asked.

"Well, I've heard that when a person is on TV, the most flattering colour for them to wear is blue. So blue it is."

Marshall laughed. "I knew better than to ask."

When Tessy hung up the phone she looked over at her cold cup of coffee. "Well, Dermot, me love, I guess that is the answer I've been waiting for. Thank ye. Ye just never let me down. God love ye."

Tessy had to get a few things done before she headed over to the Tuckers. She made herself a couple of eggs and a piece of toast for breakfast as she wanted to make sure her tummy wouldn't growl while on Skype. She bent down to put the toaster away when she blurted out, "Whoop-tuddy! My, I certainly wish I had made a better choice other than chili last night. Had I known the last twelve hours were going to turn out as they have, I certainly would have eaten something else!" she said, shaking her head. "Well, I'll be havin' a cup of fennel caraway tea before I go anywhere today," she promised herself.

Sarah greeted Tessy at the door around 10:15 a.m., and she walked in to find the atmosphere all abuzz. They had set up the computer in the living room so everyone could participate. To have the collective Tayses all joined together at one time was very rare indeed. Marshall was oblivious to Tessy even being present in the room. He was sitting in front of the computer while Jim was hooking up cords at the back and handing them down to Matt, who was under the table. It appeared to be quite an intricate operation. She remained silent for a time, then she surmised, "Gracious! Looks like the Minister of Defense will be here at any moment."

Marshall swung around with surprise. "Tessy, darling. When did you get here?" He got up and gave her a hug and kiss, then ran back to the computer as if it would disappear if he weren't there to guard it.

"A few minutes ago," she laughed. "You three definitely look like you are engrossed in a secret mission, so I'll just take myself to the kitchen to see if Penny needs any help." Not one of them acknowledged her comment or her exit.

Chuckling and shaking her head, she entered the kitchen to find Penny busy tidying up and putting the breakfast dishes in the dishwasher.

"Oh Tessy!" she cried, wiping her hands on her apron so she could give her a hug, "I'm sorry. I didn't hear you come in."

"Aye, I seem to be having that reaction everywhere I go this mornin'. No worries," she laughed.

"Can I get you a cup of coffee?" Penny offered.

"Oh, no thank ye. I've had enough of those this morning."

"A tea, then?"

"I've had one of those this morning, too. Thank ye, maybe later, dear. I'm going to float away if I have any more liquid. Not sure as it is, how I'm going to make it through the Skype without havin' to excuse myself," she chuckled.

"I'm so excited about seeing and talking to all my siblings. It's been quite a while. We decided today would be a good day as it won't be as busy as on Christmas Day or New Year's Eve. We shouldn't have any trouble getting through to everyone. Dad is almost beside himself. Between looking forward to talking to all of them and introducing you, he's been like a fidgety little boy all morning."

Aye, that and other things. Tessy grinned. "Aye, it will be grand to finally meet the others. I hope this is not going to be too big of a shock? Any type of warning ye'd like to pass on to me before we get started?"

Penny laughed. "No, I don't think so. Maybe my youngest sister, Kellie, one of the twins, might have a slight meltdown. She's our little princess – the drama queen of the family. But Dad can handle her, and the rest of us just roll our eyes, shake our heads and laugh.

Although I'm sure she'll be more upset about having to take a 7 a.m. call the morning after New Year's Eve. She's in Hawaii at the moment, so she'll be grumpy right off the get go." Penny laughed again.

"Oh my! That doesn't sound good. Poor dear," Tessy sympathetically sighed.

"Oh, sorry, Tessy. I didn't mean to worry you. It'll be just fine. Wait and see. Besides, she does it to herself. It is her choice to be in Hawaii right now. She could have had time off and come here for Christmas, so you don't need to poor dear her. Love her just the same, though. It really is quite amusing and the rest of us are so used to it. Don't give it another thought." Penny put her arm around Tessy and gave her a quick squeeze.

"Thank ye, dear," Tessy patted her hand. "Now, let me see if I have everyone straight. You're the oldest. Brian is next and lives with his little family in Switzerland. An architect, I understand. Then we have Janie, the geologist. Where is she at the moment?"

"I believe she is in Brazil on an expedition," Penny said, biting her bottom lip slightly and looking into the distance trying to remember.

"Oh my! How exciting."

"She's our quiet one. She feels rocks have more personality than most people." Penny chuckled.

"She just might be on to something when it comes to some people." Tessy laughed. "Then that leaves the twins, Kyle and Kellie, right? I know where Kellie is, but what does she do again?"

"She's a flight attendant. Hence, being in exotic places, like Hawaii, at the drop of a hat. She's really quite good at it and has the personality for it. Now that I think of it, it's about the only thing she shows any responsibility toward. That, and she's really cute!"

"No more so than you, I would think," offered Tessy. "And Kyle, he's the young doctor that has taken after your father, correct?"

"Yes. We are all so proud of him. But I wish he wouldn't spend so much time practicing in third-world countries. I know it needs to be done, but we all worry about him so much."

"Aye, a noble thing, for sure, but very worrisome."

They chatted for a bit longer, then heard the boys calling to them from the living room. They entered to find them staring at the computer screen and looking as proud as punch with themselves. It was up and running.

"Good job, guys!" Penny congratulated them.

"Now, Tessy, you come and sit in the front right here by me," Marshall instructed.

"Oh, Marshall, dear. I think you and Penny should be sitting there, especially to start with. I'll join in later after you've had a grand visit with your family," Tessy said, shaking her head. "Besides, I think ye better drop the bombshell before they get a glance at me and wonder who the heck I am."

Marshall laughed. "I suppose that would be the best thing to do. You're right. But they do know we've been seeing one another for quite some time. So I can't think they're going to be that surprised."

"Well, let's just see the reaction first. Introductions can come later," Tessy winced.

"Relax, Tessy." Marshall hugged her and rocked her back and forth for a few seconds. "Everything will be just fine." Being that close triggered the memory of their intimate evening. Marshall broke away before he accidentally disclosed their little secret.

Tessy giggled.

"Okay, bathroom break, everyone," Penny called to the troops.

Soon everyone was gathered around the computer. It was 11 a.m. Things started happening and all of a sudden faces began popping up on the screen.

"Oh my, look at that," Tessy leaned over and whispered to Sarah.

Everyone was talking at once, greeting one another and laughing. Marshall automatically took over as the spokesperson.

"Happy New Year, all! Sure good to see you guys. You look great," he started.

"Hi, Dad! Happy New Year, Dad! Good to see you too, Dad!" were the replies.

"Hi, Daddy! Love you. But couldn't you have picked a better time? Do you realize what time it is here? I just got in an hour ago!"

Tessy didn't even have to ask who that was.

Then her siblings started in. "Ooooh… poor little Kellie! Didn't you get enough beauty sleep?"

"Shut up you guys!" the tussled, tired looking Kellie pouted. Everyone laughed.

"Okay, you guys. That's enough. Leave your sister alone," Marshall smiled. "Kellie, this was the most convenient time we could all come up with, so just bear with us sweetheart."

Tessy sat back and enjoyed the family bantering that carried on for some time. Then Brian's wife and children took turns to visit with their in-laws, grandpa and cousins. It was quite a commotion for a while. There was finally a bit of a lull in the conversation and that is when Marshall cleared his throat and said he had an announcement to make.

"As you all know, I have been dating a wonderful woman by the name of Tessy McGuigan. And I think it is past due that you meet her. Tessy, please join me." Penny got up and Marshall held out his hand and guided Tessy to the chair beside him. She was wearing a lovely indigo blue, bohemian style top. "Kids, this is Tessy." Tessy bashfully smiled and waved to everyone. "Tessy, this handsome fellow is my oldest son, Brian," he said as he pointed to the upper portion of the screen with pride.

"Brian, 'tis a pleasure to finally meet ye," Tessy said as she gazed into his face.

"You, too, Tessy. What's a nice girl like you doing with an old boot like him?" Brian teased.

Tessy laughed and nudged up against Marshall while he retorted, "Hah! Just remember you are my offspring and not getting any younger yourself."

Marshall then turned his attention to his daughter, Janie. "Tessy, this is my gem, Janie."

"Hello, Janie, dear. I hear ye are a geologist and have quite a passion towards the rock people. I, too, have that passion and can't wait for ye to study my collection. We will have much to share, I'm sure."

"Wow! Really? Yeah, I'd love to do that sometime, nice to meet you. Way to go, Dad!"

Everyone laughed.

"Well, darling. I think you have her vote," Marshall leaned and quietly whispered to Tessy.

"Kyle, you're next. Still awake, son? I know it's been a long day for you. Tessy, this is Dr. Kyle Tayse. Presently practicing in Tanzania."

"Well, another Dr. Tayse, very nice to meet ye, Kyle. What a wonderful service ye are providing for those lucky people who have ye there. Just be sure ye take care of yourself as well. You're a long way from home. How much longer is it that ye'll be over there?"

"Hi Tessy, nice to meet you, too. I should be here another four to five months. Then I'll head home and stay there for a while, probably with Dad."

"Oh, thanks for the heads-up!" Marshall laughed. "Looking forward to it, son."

"Last, and certainly not least, is my baby, Kellie," Marshall teased his youngest.

"Kellie, dear, how nice to meet ye. So, ye're in beautiful Hawaii, are ye? Have ye been out to see some of the wondrous sites yet? Pearl Harbor or maybe Nuusnau Pali Lookout? Fantastic views from there."

"Hi. Yeah, sightseeing… not really my thing," Kellie said as she scrunched up her face.

"Yeah, culture is not really high on Kellie's list. Laying on a beach somewhere is more her speed," quipped her oldest brother.

"Yeah, with a Mai Tai in each hand," Kyle added, laughing.

"Daddy, tell them to stop teasing me or I'm going to go," Kellie whined.

"Okay, you guys. Cut it out. And Kellie, stop being so sensitive. Is what they are saying anything that isn't true?"

"No. But they don't have to always laugh at me. I have to be able to recommend good beaches and stuff to my passengers when they ask. It's part of my job."

"Ooooh… market research. Is that what they call it, sis?" Kyle just couldn't resist.

"Enough!" Marshall waved his hands in the air. "I want to make a very important announcement. Kids, I have asked Tessy to marry me. And we are hoping we have your blessings."

Everyone went silent.

Tessy looked to Marshall for support. He smiled and kissed her hand.

Penny jumped in. "Well, you two sure have our blessings. We could not be happier. Okay, you guys… say something."

"Wow! Dad, Tessy… Congratulations!" Brian was the next to speak.

"Hey, great news!" added Janie.

"When's the big day?" Kyle inquired.

"Daddy! How could you do this to us? No offence, Terry, but Daddy, we don't even know her. What about Mom?" was Kellie's tearful response.

"It's Tessy, honey. And I'm not doing anything to any of you. We love one another very much and we want to spend the rest of our lives together, with or without your blessing. Make an effort and come and get to know her. And, for your information, your mother wanted me to go on to live and love again. In fact, she insisted on it, but I didn't think it was possible. Until now." Marshall smiled at Tessy and squeezed her hand.

"Kellie, dear, I know this is a bit of a shock for ye all. I truly love and care for your father very much, but that doesn't mean I'm trying to replace your mother. No one can replace another person, especially when ye've loved that other person whom ye have had five beautiful children with. Please, just give me a chance and don't be too hard on your father. We are so very happy," Tessy pleaded.

Then Penny spoke up, "Kellie, don't you dare do this. Tessy is wonderful and we all love her so much. The next time you have a stopover in Regina you can come out here for a few days and spend some time getting to know her. Or maybe next time you're in Winnipeg, Dad can have Tessy come stay, too. Something, anything, but do not put a wrench into their plans."

"Oh, all right. Everybody stop picking on me," Kellie grumbled.

"Thank you, everyone. We haven't made any plans, as of yet, as this just happened a few days ago. So as soon as we know any details we'll let you know. I am very happy and I want all of you to be happy for me, too. I love each and every one of you, and I know that each and every one of you will grow to love Tessy as much as we do here."

Janie, the quiet one, spoke. "Well, Dad, most of us are already okay with it. If Tessy makes you that happy, then we're happy, too. Welcome to the family, Tessy."

"Ditto!" Brian smiled.

"You bet; welcome to the mayhem!" Kyle chuckled.

Penny, using her strictest mother voice, added, "Kellie, do you have something you'd like to say?"

"I guess. Congratulations, Daddy," she sighed.

"Again, thank you everyone. Well, it's pretty late in Tanzania and pretty early in Hawaii so I guess we should wrap this up for now. Sure great seeing and talking to you. Take care of yourselves and stay in touch. Love you all. Bye for now."

"Bye, Dad! Bye everybody."

"See ya Dad, take care. Bye guys!"

"Bye, Dad, love you. Bye Tessy. Looking forward to getting to know you. Make sure to keep those rocks polished."

"Bye, Daddy."

"Bye, Kellie. Get some sleep, kitten."

Then the screen went blank and all was quiet.

"Phew! Well, that didn't go so badly." Marshall wiped the back of his hand across his brow.

"Were you really that worried?" Tessy asked.

"I'd be lying if I said I wasn't a little nervous. I guess it is pretty big news. But the aftermath wasn't as bad as I thought," he replied honestly.

"Thanks for sharing that with me now. Although, I really don't think I would have wanted to learn that any earlier!" she laughed.

The rest of the day was spent with the kids out in the snow. It was too cold to make a snowman or to have a good, old-fashioned snowball fight, but it was perfect for tobogganing.

Everyone bundled up and off they went to spend an afternoon of fun on Hobbs Hill.

5
Departed Betrothed

The next morning, Marshall said his good-byes to his family, put the last of his luggage in the SUV, and backed out of the driveway. He was feeling pretty grim. Each time he left it was a little more difficult than the last. He really wasn't looking forward to his next stop – Ashling Manor.

Tessy was expecting him and stood waiting, looking out the lace curtains which hung on her large, oak front door. When she saw him coming up the front steps she sadly pulled it open.

"Good mornin', love." she greeted him with as much enthusiasm as she could.

"Good morning, sweetheart," Marshall sighed and leaned down to hold her.

"Now, don't ye be gettin' all long in the jaw," Tessy scolded. "We'll be together again in the wink of an eye, ye'll see. This is going to be a difficult time for all of us, but we have to stay as positive as possible."

"Oh Tessy! I don't want to go. I don't want to leave you, my family, this is so hard."

"Marshall, dear. This is the way it has to be for now. You have a wonderful practice in Winnipeg with patients that need ye and are waiting for ye. That has to be your focus right at the moment. It's not going to be that way forever. I love you so much, dear. I hate to see you being pulled apart every time ye leave, so we have to make it work. We will make this work." Tessy smiled and gently touched his cheek with the palm of her hand, then hugged him.

"Thank you, sweetheart. I really needed to hear that. Yes, we will make this work. I will stop wallowing in despair and do what has to be done," he said, then pulled away from Tessy and held her cheeks in both his hands. "But it doesn't make it any easier or mean I'm going to miss you any less," he added.

"Aye, nor I, you. Do ye still keep that wee travel protection pouch I made up for ye in your glove compartment?"

"Yes, it's still in there, dear. And I appreciate it. Thank you."

"Grand. That makes me feel better. Well now, ye have a long drive ahead of you and on roads that won't be so pleasant in some spots, so you better be off with ye." Tessy fussed with his scarf and patted his lapel, trying to hide the tears that were so very close to the surface.

"Well, Tessy McGuigan. I arrived in Ladyslipper a single man and I am leaving the happiest engaged man on the face of the earth." He picked up her hands and kissed them. "Thank you."

"Thank ye? For what are ye thanking me? I am the other half of that happy engagement ye're talking about," she chuckled.

Marshall laughed. "Oh, Tessy… you are a magical wonder… and also a very wise woman! All right, I'm going. I love you with all my heart. I will call you as soon as I step in the door at home." He kissed her again and again.

"Now be off with ye before ye start something ye can't finish." She playfully slapped his chest.

"Oooooh, don't go there, my lady. I would be more than happy to stay and finish whatever gets started." Marshall's impish smile and twinkling blue eyes were almost too much for Tessy to resist.

"Out with ye!" she giggled. "And say hi to Dotty and Bert for me. I'm certainly glad they are there to look after ye. St. Paddy, himself, would only know what kind of trouble ye'd get into without them."

Marshall bent down and kissed her. "I love you," he said as he opened the door and stepped outside.

Tessy flung her large cable-knit shawl around her shoulders and stepped out on to the veranda to watch and wave good-bye to her betrothed. As she caught the last glimpse of his taillights turning out of the lane she sighed, wiped a tear from her cheek, and felt a little pang in her chest. *Oh my, I do love that man.* Somehow this was different, more urgent, and more passionate than she remembered with her beloved Dermot. With Dermot, it was always so sweet, easy and comfortable. There just didn't seem to be anything easy about this relationship. The distance, the excitement, the importance of every moment they spent together, and the longing. Yes, this was a little more complex. However, after being Tessy McGuigan for so many years, was she really sure she was ready to completely give that up? So many things to contemplate, but not at this moment, she mused.

Tessy gave her head a shake and went back into the house. She went down the hall and into the library to have a chat with Dermot. "Well, Dermot, my love, I wish ye could tell me what the plan was that we agreed to on the other side before we came to be on this earth. I know it was simple at the time, but it seems to have become a touch complicated for me since then. You, being back there, remember what it is, but I'm not quite so fortunate. Well, keep me posted when ye can. I'll be here listening for any wee whispers ye might want to share with me. God bless ye."

For the remainder of the day, Tessy busied herself with putting the rest of her Christmas decorations away. Marshall and the kids had helped her undecorate the tree and haul it out to end of the lane a couple of days ago. She looked around; most traces of Christmas were gone. There were still some floral arrangements and the odd little winter knick-knack to make things feel warm and cozy, for which she was grateful. It was late afternoon and she was just returning from carting the last plastic bin of decorations to the attic when the phone rang. She ran down the hall and picked it up on the third ring.

"Yes, hello, hello!" she puffed.

"Tessy? Are you all right? What's the matter?" It was Marshall sounding extremely concerned.

"Aye, love, yes. I'm just fine now. How was ye're trip, dear?"

"Where did I get you from?" Marshall continued.

"Oh, love, just down from the attic, is all. I'm as fine as frog's fur," she chuckled.

"Oh, good! You had me worried. I was about ready to jump in the car and head back out to you." Marshall sounded relieved.

"Sorry, dear. Now, how was your trip?"

"It was good until around Portage la Prairie, then it turned pretty nasty for a while. Snowing and blowing across the highway so bad some parts were a complete whiteout. But here I am, safe and sound. Thanks to your protection pouch, I'm sure."

"Were Dotty and Bert there to welcome ye?"

"Yes," Marshall laughed. "Dotty has a pot roast with all the trimmings in the slow cooker waiting for us to enjoy, and she just poured me a very welcomed scotch, which I plan on finishing before dinner."

"Well, love, thank ye so much for calling and putting my fears to rest. I'll let ye go. I'm sure ye must be exhausted. Have a nice evening and a good night's sleep," Tessy cooed.

"Thank you, sweetheart. The only thing that would make it better is if you were here in my arms. I miss you and I love you."

"Soon, love, soon. I love ye, too. Give my best to Dotty and Bert. Good night, then."

"Good night, sweetheart."

Tessy hung up the phone and exhaled a huge sigh of relief.

6
Wise Women 101

Sarah and Cherokee were coming over to start their lessons. Tessy wanted them to begin before any more misconceptions occurred. She was bundling her sage and lavender, preparing for a cleansing smudge, when the girls came clamouring to the back door. Their excitement to get started was quite apparent.

"Morning, Tessy," they chimed as they walked in.

"Aye, mornin' girls. And what a grand one it is. It certainly sounds like you're anxious to get going."

"Yes! We can't wait. Where do you want us to put our kits?" Cherokee asked, looking around.

"Well, if you each pick a side of the table and open out your kits, that would be grand. It's wonderful to see ye so eager, but we must calm ourselves," she said, smiling and shaking her head.

The girls giggled. "Yes, ma'am."

"Now, before we begin, can I get either of ye anything?"

"No. I'm fine, thanks," Sarah answered, shooting Cherokee a look.

"Nope. Me either, thanks," Cherokee added.

"All right, then. Let's get started. Today's lesson will be mostly showing you how to cleanse and prepare your space. Most times, I like to start by performing a smudge. Cherokee, coming from a long line of shamans, I know ye're familiar with this practice. My favourite combination is sage and lavender, and for lighting it I like to use a wooden match."

"Wouldn't it be easier to just use a lighter?" Sarah asked.

"Aye, maybe, and plenty of people do, but I just don't like releasing the chemicals into the space."

"Good point. Makes sense," Cherokee agreed as both girls nodded.

"Sarah, if ye'd like to hold the bundle over this Abalone shell while Cherokee lights it. Then place it in the shell once it is lit and smoking. Now, take this feather fan and I'll show you how to sweep the smoke."

The girls very carefully did as they were instructed.

"Very good. Now, I'll crack open the door a mite so the stale energy is let out. Grand. Now make your way around the kitchen being sure to get in all the wee nooks and crannies. Another way to easily cleanse your space, if ye don't have any herbs on hand or ye're in a bit of a rush, is to simply clap your hands to shake up any stagnant energy. Making sure, once again, to get into all the corners. Then take a broom, specifically for that purpose, and sweep all the loosened stale energy out the door."

"Cool!" the girls echoed. They walked around the kitchen, taking turns, sweeping the smoke through the air, stopping occasionally to re-light the herbs.

Once Tessy was satisfied with the cleansing, she asked them to set down the shell and take out their kit of crystals and gems.

"Now, there are two ways for ye to use your crystals. First, ye can quiet yourself and listen to hear which crystals speak to ye, or ye can choose your stones by their individual characteristic or purpose. Today, I think we shall see which ones speak to ye, as we still need to study more on characteristics. Please, take your time, girls."

The girls methodically contemplated over their choices and placed them on the table.

Tessy was thrilled. "A grand selection, girls! Very nice." It was plain to see the girls each had a natural gift in the healing arts.

"Next, we light our candles and call in all angels, spirits and deities. Again, ye can ask all that want to attend to be here today, or ye can ask for specific healing entities. Today, we ask for those who wish to be here with us."

"How do we know who to ask for?" Sarah questioned.

Tessy chuckled. "Again, it is study, learn and feel."

"To be an herbalist, are all of these steps necessary?" Sarah asked.

"No. If ye feel that your medicine is potent enough without, of course ye may do so."

"Would you make any without a cleansing, Tessy?" Cherokee quizzed.

"You'll come to naturally know when it is necessary for a cleansing, but it never hurts to do one regardless," Tessy answered honestly.

"Boy, there sure is a lot to learn," Sarah exhaled.

"Aye. They say it takes seven lifetimes to become a true herbalist."

"What!" The girls chimed.

Tessy laughed. "I've found the more I learn about Mother Earth and her plants, the more there is to learn. Being an herbalist is not necessarily someone who knows uses for fifty herbs but someone who knows fifty uses for one herb."

"Really? That's a cool way to look at it," said Sarah.

"Aye. Nature can teach us so much if we just stop and pay attention. As a student healer, what ye learn from me is merely the first step on your journey. The bulk of it will come from experiencing the practical use, acquiring the confidence to do so, and a great deal of intuition. You will come to realize that you are the tool the Divine and the Universe has chosen to use. You will receive the wisdom, guidance and the energy from above."

Since today's lesson was focusing more on preparation, Tessy decided to just spend some time introducing the girls to various herbs. Being January in Saskatchewan, the only fresh herbs she had were the culinary ones she had planted and which were now sitting in her kitchen windowsill. She got the girls to carry them over to the table while she went in to her back kitchen and brought out a tray of mason jars filled with dried herbs. Tessy had Sarah and Cherokee touch, smell, taste and make notes on their findings. Next, they made samples of teas, first with individual herbs; then they were told to get creative and make some blends they thought would work well together, mostly for taste at this point in time. Again, Tessy was very impressed as to what the girls came up with.

"Very nice, ladies. More often than not, ye'll find a medicine has to taste good for a patient to want to take it," she chuckled.

"That makes perfect sense," Cherokee nodded.

"Well, I think we've had a grand start, but now it's lunch time. I've had a hearty soup brewing all mornin'. Would ye like to stay for a bowl?"

Both girls eagerly accepted.

"All right, then. Let's get this table cleaned off. But first, we must blow out the candles and thank all the angels, spirits and deities for accompanying us here today."

While they enjoyed their meal, the girls quizzed Tessy.

"You usually listen to music while you prepare your creations, don't you?" Cherokee questioned between bites.

"Aye. I do. If I'm preparing a relaxing or calming medicine, then I listen to something soft and easy like… Zen. If it's something exhilarating I'm after, then possibly a lively Celtic ditty would work, and if it's a magical effect I'm needin' then there is nothing like the ancient, spiritual sound of the native flutes and drums. Music can take you to the higher realms like no other. But, there again, some people prefer to work in silence. It just remains a personal preference."

Sarah paused and said, "Tessy, you said that you repeated a chant when you made that stuff for Grandma."

"Aye. I did," Tessy replied.

"Do you always say a chant when you prepare something like that?"

"Aye, most of the time."

"Should we be saying a chant?"

"Sarah, dear, your intent is always what is most important."

"Then why do you say the chant?"

Tessy laughed. "Well, I guess, for me, it enhances the intent and shows respect for my belief system."

"Oh. That's the study, learn and feel thing you were talking about, right?"

"Aye, dear. You will find your own way when the time is right."

7
A New Purchase Leads to a New Friend

Tessy was busy reading through all her Christmas cards and letters, one more time before she packed them away, when she discovered the gift certificate that Jim and the staff at the pharmacy had given her. "Blessed be! Almost tucked ye away." It was a gift certificate for one of her favourite spots, the local garden center, Nurturing Nature. Seeing it, she got excited all over again. "Bless their hearts for thinking of me and in such a thoughtful manner." She decided she would get ready and head down to Nurturing Nature straight away. She wanted to put it toward a lovely, large, indoor water fountain she'd had her eye on for some time which she thought would look wonderful in her front foyer.

It was mid-January and Tessy hadn't been in the garden center since early December, so she was quite surprised to see they had received a new shipment of fountains. Her work was cut out for her now! They still had the original one she had liked but… *look at these new ones,* she thought as she sauntered up and down the aisles pondering over the recent additions. It was a taxing decision, but after about forty-five minutes Tessy had made her choice.

"It's a lovely piece, Tessy," Clare, the storeowner, congratulated Tessy on her decision.

"Aye, it is. I think it will look grand in the spot I've picked."

"Well, I will have my husband, Gary, and our hired hand, Tommy, drop it off tomorrow around 10 a.m."

"That sounds wonderful, Clare. Thank ye kindly."

Tessy was up early the next morning to do her meditation and yoga routine. She was just finishing up when the phone rang.

"Good mornin' to ye," she greeted.

"Good morning to you as well, my sweet lady," Marshall returned.

"Dr. Tayse! My, you're up with the birds this mornin'."

"Yeah, afraid so. I have a patient I need to stop in and see at the hospital before I go into the office."

"Oh. Nothing too serious, I hope."

"Hopefully not. But that's why I'd like to check in and make sure."

"Oh, my. Well, I'll be sending ye some prayers and positive energy your way."

"Thanks, honey. But, I actually called to see if you could make it out here for Valentine's Day weekend or for however long you'd like to stay? Longer the better, as far as I'm concerned."

"My, that would be lovely, wouldn't it? And I believe the Festival du Voyageur is on during that time, as well."

"Yes, I believe that's right. So is that a yes?"

"I'll take a look at my schedule this week when I go in to the pharmacy and let you know."

"That would be great. I'd like to get your flight booked as soon as possible."

"Now, Marshall, ye don't have to be buying me anything. That includes tickets. The trip to Ireland ye have booked for us is more than enough. I can pay my own way."

"We are not even going there, Tessy. Consider it part of your Valentine's gift."

"Marshall Tayse, ye are an impossible man."

"Maybe so, my lady, but you're stuck with me now," Marshall chuckled.

"Aye. I suppose I am. And glad of it, love."

"Well, I had better get going, Tess. I'll talk to you as soon as you find out about Valentine's."

"All right, dear. Have a grand day and blessings with your dear patient."

"Thanks, honey. Bye."

Tessy hung up, smiling and shaking her head. What a dear man he is. I am so blessed. She immediately went back into meditation to send positive energy out to where it was needed.

About 9 a.m., Tessy went into the foyer to move things around and make room for her new purchase.

"Oh, grand! There is an electrical outlet on this wall," she said out loud as she moved the small table that was there. She took her mop and gave the area a good wiping. With the fountain being so large and heavy it would be a long while before that was likely to be done again.

About an hour later there was a knock at the door.

"Morning, Tessy," Gary greeted her.

"Mornin', Gary. And how are ye this fine day?"

"Great, thanks. Where would you like Tommy and I to put this beauty?"

"Oh, right over against that far wall, please."

They carefully wheeled in a trolley with the large structure balanced just so and gently set it down in place. They then maneuvered it until it was flush against the wall, leaving just enough room for Tessy to reach the outlet.

Tommy hung his head a little and smiled. "Looks very nice, Ms. McGuigan." He then tipped his hat and walked back out to the delivery truck.

My, it does look grand! Tessy was so pleased. "Thank ye kindly, Gary. I'd like to give you and your hand a little something for your troubles."

"Not necessary for me, Tessy, but I'm sure Tommy could use a little something, if you'd like. Poor fellow just moved here the end of November and doesn't have much. We were so busy in December and needed some help but now, being January, things really slow down and I don't think we can keep him on much longer. If you happen to hear of anyone looking for a good hand, please let us know. He's been clearing sidewalks for a little extra cash."

"That's where I've seen him!" Tessy clapped her hands together. "And I believe he was the young chap that delivered a Christmas arrangement to me last month. Aye, I'll definitely keep my ears tuned. Well, here. Could ye please pass this on to the lad, then?"

"You bet, Tessy. And thanks," he smiled as he held up the bill she had handed him.

For the remainder of the morning Tessy artfully placed houseplants and whimsical knickknacks on and around the fountain. When she had it full of water and everything arranged as she wanted, she plugged it in. It was spectacular! The sound, the smell, the energy, all were amazing. The water fell from the flat part of the six-foot structure that hugged the wall and collected in a large rustic bowl with a ledge wide enough to set some fresh greenery and the odd faery figurine. She noticed some water was splashing out on one side, but removing a couple of cups of water soon fixed that problem. She stood there admiring it for quite some time. Her two cats, Merlin and Cordelia, had to come to thoroughly survey and investigate the large invasive object. They cautiously crouched and sniffed, ready to bolt at any sign of movement. Then, confidently, they rubbed up against it and finally, there was Merlin, up on the ledge, poking his nose close and taking a few laps of water.

Tessy had to laugh. "So, ye found yourself another drinkin' hole, did ye? Guess I'll not be adding any fish to it any time soon."

The next morning, Tessy decided she had better head down to the pharmacy to see how things were holding up in her Wee Nook of Herbals and Oils, and of course, to check the schedule. When she got there, Tommy was out front shoveling the walks.

"Good mornin' to ye, Tommy," Tessy greeted, stopping to chat.

"Oh, good morning, Ms. McGuigan." Tommy stopped shoveling and tipped at his tuque. "Thanks you so much for the generous tip yesterday."

"Now, Tommy, if we're going to be running into each other as often as I think we might, ye best call me Tessy, as everyone does. And you're very welcome. I appreciate the hand in gettin' that monstrosity into my house." She chuckled. "Well, I best head in. Ye have a grand day, now."

"Thank you, Ms. McGuigan… um, Tessy. You too."

Jim was standing just inside the door looking over some paperwork at the front counter when Tessy walked in.

"Mornin', Jim. What a fine young lad that Tommy is. I'm so glad ye're able to help him out by getting him to shovel the walk for us." Tessy stomped the snow off her boots.

"Morning, Tess. Yes, he sure seems to be. Hard worker, that's for certain."

Tessy made her way to the back of the store, removed her coat, and got right to work. She was down a few more products than she thought. She was making a list of the items she was short of when she heard the bells on the front door tinkle. Then Mrs. Chamberlain's distinctive voice resonating throughout the store.

"Mr. Tucker, I am surprised you would allow that bum out in front of your store."

Jim walked around the counter and went to the window to see what Mrs. Chamberlain was talking about.

"Bum. What bum?" Jim looked up and down the street. Tessy made her way to the front of the store.

"Well… well… that bum there!" She pointed at Tommy.

"Mrs. Chamberlain, that is not a bum. That is Tommy Bracken and he's doing us a great service by keeping our sidewalk cleared off." Jim shook his head.

"Well, all he does is odd jobs around town and he lives in a room at the downtown hotel, of all things!" she sniffed.

Tessy jumped in. "Mrs. Chamberlain, Tommy is not a bum. He's just a little down on his luck, is all. And he's willing to do an honest day's work for a little pay. I can't think of anything more honourable."

"Oh, for heaven's sake. What do you know? You'd let anyone settle in Ladyslipper." She turned to Jim. "Mr. Tucker, I've come to pick up my prescription for the pain in my ankle. It just won't stop hurting so I hope these pills work."

"This prescription should help, Mrs. Chamberlain, but I would also like to suggest that you try some of Tessy's joint cream. It has done wonders for some of my other customers."

"You have to be joking!" she huffed. "I refuse to put anything that witch makes near my body. Now, my prescription please. The sooner I get it and get out of here, the better."

When she was finished and limping her way out the door, Tessy called after her, "Isn't it nice to know that the ice is all cleared off and you don't have to worry about slippin'?"

"Good day," the disgruntled woman growled.

Jim looked at Tessy after Mrs. Chambelain left and added, "I always expect that woman's attitude to change at some point in time, but I fear I shall remain disappointed." Tessy just chuckled.

Tessy had been brainstorming about Tommy's situation since her conversation yesterday with Gary. She didn't think she knew anyone who was looking for help right at the moment. All of a sudden she had an idea. She ran out the door looking for Tommy, without even putting on her coat. He had already finished up in front of the pharmacy and had moved on down the street. Tessy spotted him. "Tommy. Tommy, dear," she called waving her hands and running as quickly as she dared.

"Ms. McGuigan… er Tessy, What is it?" Tommy ran back towards her.

"Oh, Tommy," Tessy stopped to catch her breath. "I was wondering if ye could come over later this afternoon and shovel my walks and then, if ye'd like to stay and have a bite with me? I've a lovely, thick stew brewing in my crock pot and I'll make some nice sour dough biscuits to go with it."

"You bet! That sounds awesome! Thanks. Can I walk you back to the pharmacy? And here, put my scarf around your shoulders until we get there."

"Thank ye, dear." And the two new friends made their way back down the street.

Tessy couldn't wait to get home. She had a couple of phone calls to make, and hopefully, all would end well.

8

For the Good of All

About 4:30 p.m., Tommy arrived to shovel Tessy's walkway. There really wasn't much left to clear off, but he continued to clean them right down to the pavement where he could. He was just finishing up when Tessy came to the door to see how he was doing.

"A fine job you've done for me, Tommy. Thank ye. Are ye 'bout ready to come in, then?" she called.

"Yes, ma'am. Thank you."

Tommy stomped the snow off his boots outside, then took the broom that was there and brushed the snow off his pant legs before going in. The smells were amazing! He hadn't had much to eat that day and his stomach was letting him know. He carefully removed his tuque, mitts, scarf and coat so as not to get any snow on Tessy's floor, and hung them up on the hooks in the foyer. Tessy had gone into the kitchen to check on supper and he was not quite sure what he was to do or where to go. Thankfully, Tessy came scurrying back down the hallway to rescue him.

"Come in. Come in, dear. Follow me into the kitchen. Ye can warm up there and we can have a wee nibble on some snacks I've prepared."

"Thank you, Ms. McGuigan… um… Tessy," the bashful young man replied. "Boy, your water fountain sure looks great. I love all the accents you've added. Looks like it was just plucked out of the forest and set in your foyer." He smiled.

"Well, thank ye kindly. I have really been enjoying it, for sure."

Tommy was walking past Tessy to go and sit at the kitchen table when his stomach loudly growled. "Excuse me," he blushed.

"Ye just never mind, now. Go help yourself to some of the fixin's on the table. Would ye like a hot drink or maybe ye'd like a Guinness. I used some in my stew, and when I do that I always buy a few extra. Being Irish and all, I've been known to tip the odd one back from time to time and thought I might just treat myself tonight. Would ye like to join me?"

"Well, I don't drink much but I do like Guinness. So… sure, that sounds great. Thanks. Can I help with anything?" Tommy offered and moved to get up.

"No, no. Thank ye, dear. I'm just fine. Sit. Sit," Tessy ushered him.

Tessy took out two large cans of Guinness from the refrigerator and then two tall, glass mugs. She handed one to Tommy with his beer, then sat down at the head of the table. They each cracked open the tabs, carefully poured their brew, and when they shook the last of it into their glasses, they could hear the widget rattling in the cans.

"Sláinte." Tessy held up her glass to Tommy and the two new friends toasted before they each took a generous gulp.

Tessy said it all with an "Ahhh," then added, "Not quite as good as the dark brew over in Ireland but pretty good, nonetheless."

"Is it different over there?" Tommy asked.

"Aye. For some reason, I find it is. Not quite sure why, maybe it just tastes better being in my homeland."

"I've never been to Ireland, but I sure would love to see it someday," Tommy dreamily wished as he reached for some cheese to put on his cracker.

"Never give up on your dreams, Tommy."

"Well, I try not to but they seem to give up on me," he said, while trying to make a choice as to which cold cut to add on his cheese and cracker.

"Oh, Tommy. I hate to hear ye say that. Dreams do have a way of coming true if ye just hold to them. I know it doesn't always seem that way, but our journey eventually shows us the lessons we have to learn, and they do make us stronger.

"I guess. I just wish I knew what I was supposed to be learning so I could get this part of the lesson over with."

"If ye don't mind me askin', how is it ye arrived here in Ladyslipper?"

"I was on the bus on my way to Alberta, and this is as far as my money got me. I came from New Brunswick."

"Oh, New Brunswick, is it? What a beautiful part of Canada that is. So that's where your family's from, then?"

"Yes, it is beautiful, but it was just me and my Mom. She died eight months ago. When she got really sick I dropped out of my mechanics course and moved back home to help out as much as I could. We didn't have much and everything we did have went towards medical bills, then her burial." Tommy put his head down and was quiet for a moment. He quickly brushed a tear away.

Tessy's heart was breaking for this sweet boy who seemed to be carrying the weight of the world. She got up and put her hand on his heavy shoulders and gently rubbed them. "I'm so sorry, Tommy. It must be so hard for you. I know what it is like to lose someone ye love very much. Is there no one else ye can turn to?"

"Nope. I never knew my dad, and my grandparents are gone as well." He bravely smiled up at Tessy.

"Well, your mam raised a fine young man and I know she's so proud of ye and watching over ye every minute. We're blessed that ye made it this far. And believe it or not, this is where you are meant to be right at this moment in time. 'Tis all for a reason."

"Thank you, Tessy. I suppose. I really do like Ladyslipper, but I'm not sure I will be able to stay if I can't find any full time work."

"Well, Tommy, dear, that is another reason I asked ye to join me tonight. Hopefully, we'll be able to fix that wee problem for ye."

"What do you mean, Tessy?"

"Don't know if ye know my neighbour across the way, Danny Baker, and his lovely wife, Betty. Well, Danny has a good size farm, and with his sciatica acting up lately he needs a hand. Right at the moment, he is to be collecting all the used Christmas trees around town and bringing them back to his farm to mulch up and sell in the spring. They have a cozy bunkhouse on the far side of the farmyard with a large wood stove to keep ye toasty. I talked to Danny earlier today, and he said he would be glad to talk to you tomorrow and see what the two of ye think. And, oh, Betty's cookin' is second to none! She'll keep ye as plump as a hen, she will."

Tommy was stupefied for a moment. "Oh, Ms. McGuigan… Tessy. I… I… don't know what to say. Thank you so much. That sounds wonderful. I've always been good on the farm. That's actually what I was doing just before Mom passed away. I was taking farm mechanics. This is like a dream come true. Thank you." He ran his hand through his hair and put his head down while slowly shaking it.

"Oh, ye are very welcome, dear," Tessy chuckled. "It won't be me getting ye the job tomorrow. It will be you. And Danny Baker will make ye work for your supper."

"Yes, ma'am. I promise to do my best and not disappoint you."

"Ye'll never be a disappointment, dear. Now, eat up some of these snacks I've made for ye, and then we can concentrate on a fine Irish stew. Sláinte." She held up her mug, they tapped their glasses, and each took another generous gulp in celebration.

9
A Cleansing and Clearing

Things had slowed down enough at the pharmacy for Tessy to let Marshall know that she would be able to make the trip to Winnipeg for ten days mid-February. This ensured that she would not miss one of her favourite events there, Festival du Voyageur. Marshall was thrilled and immediately booked her trip.

February may be the shortest month of the year, but it was a very important one to Tessy. It is the month of the first Sabbat of the New Year, Imbolc; her and her twin brother, Keenan's, birthday; and Valentine's Day, the day of love.

In Canadian tradition, February 2nd is known as Ground Hog Day. It is the day that Nature reassures us that spring is really on its way. The Celtic tradition of Imbolc is also observed on February 2nd and is not so dissimilar. It is a time to celebrate the renewing fertility of the Earth. As Imbolc is the seed that starts the wheel of the year turning, there is a feeling that spring is coming and possibilities are endless. It is a time to clean up and clear out anything that might hinder the planting that will soon begin. It is also a time of hearth and home, time for purification and cleansing of one's mental, physical, spiritual and emotional being. This is when Tessy does her *magical* housekeeping. She cleans with earth-friendly products, mostly homemade with essential oils and flower essences. On nice, sunny days she opens up the doors to let out the long winter's stale air, then she does space clearing with clapping and smudging. Next is a broom blessing, and then she uses a number of different magical floor washes to freshen and sparkle up her floors. These particular rituals always brighten Tessy's winter season, leaving her so invigorated.

Tessy was just finishing up with one of her spare bedroom floors when her thoughts turned to her forthcoming trip to Winnipeg. Knowing her birthday was going to fall while she was there, she was a little concerned as to how she and Marshall would be celebrating it. She didn't want Marshall to make any kind of fuss, but knowing that dear, sweet, generous man, only St. Paddy himself knew what kind of shenanigans he would have up his sleeve. She also decided that since she always talks to her twin brother, Keenan, on their birthday, she would call him before she left so they could have a real good visit in private. Ireland is seven hours ahead, so if she called him tomorrow morning around 10 a.m. he should be getting in for a pint before supper about then. "Aye, that will be a fine time to catch him," she said to Cordelia, who had just come in to inspect Tessy's clean floor.

The next morning, Tessy busily scurried about until 10:10 a.m. She then poured herself a tea, picked up the phone, and began dialing a great many numbers. It was picked up on the third ring. "Good evenin' to ye," was the response.

"Keenan, dear? Is that ye?" Tessy called out, not sure whether the connection was clear.

"Aye. Tessy?" Keenan questioned.

"Aye. How are ye fairing?"

"I'm doin' fine. How are ye? What are ye calling for? Are ye all right?" He sounded concerned.

"Aye, dear. Just as fine as frog's fur, I am. I just thought I'd call a few days early as I'm going to be away on the eleventh."

"Away, are ye? And where are ye off to, then?"

"I'm going to Winnipeg to spend some time with Marshall and hopefully see Auntie Shannon while I'm there."

"Grand. I'll be lookin' forward to meetin' the man that's got ye all up in a tangle. And ohhh, Auntie Shannon, how is the old gal?" Keenan chuckled.

"I think she's doing well. When I saw her last, at Thanksgiving, she was going on about her time passin', and she had a wee parcel from Mam for me. It was quite unsettlin', it was."

"No kiddin'. She sent me a wee parcel, as well, and told me to not open it until she was gone and ye were there with me to open it."

"Keenan! That is exactly what I was told. What do ye think of it?"

"I'm really not sure. Mam and Dad have been gone for so many years. Why now? Do ye think we should open them straight away?"

"No! Definitely not! We made a promise and I plan on stickin' to it and so should ye!"

"Aye, I suppose. But it sure is a mystery though. When I come over for your weddin' you'll have to show me the wee box. Maybe it's exactly like mine and we can figure it out."

"So ye are plannin' on comin' to the wedding, then?"

"Of course! I'm not about to let my only sibling get married off without me tippin' a few pints and dancin' at her wedding. Besides, I have to see if this rogue you've picked is any good for my sister."

Tessy laughed. "Oh, I think the two of ye will hit it off just grand. And, ye know, you'll be the one puttin' up with us while we're over there for a month."

"Aye. And looking forward to it."

They chatted on for another twenty minutes or so until Tessy finally said, "Well, Keenan, I'll let ye get to your supper. It was grand talking to ye. Take care and have a Happy Birthday. I miss ye terribly."

"Aye, and ye too. I'll be in touch with ye soon. Hurry up and plan a date so I have something to look forward to."

"Aye. We'll probably decide that while I'm there. Say hi and my love to your Mary and all the rest. Bye for now, dear."

"Bye, Tess." And the line went quiet.

Tessy always had feelings of longing after talking to Keenan. She missed him, missed her homeland, and missed her heritage. She knew her heritage was always with her, but it somehow felt so far away from her at times like this. She took her hankie out of her apron pocket and dabbed a tear. Well, I'm not going to get down and all teary eyed. In just a few short months Keenan will be here and then I will be going home to Ireland with the man I love. What could be better than that? she scolded herself.

Tessy was packing for her trip the next day with a number of questions on her mind. She didn't deny that ten days, under one roof, would definitely be a good test to see if she and Marshall were, in fact, compatible. They hadn't spent that much time together consecutively and she was a little worried. As she packed, she was having a little conversation with her black cat. "What do ye think, Merlin? Do ye think it is all going to work out? Well, I do know that it will work the way it is supposed to, so I best stop fretting about it and let the good Lord do his work without me meddling in it. Thanks, dear," she said as she reached over and stroked his soft, gleaming black coat. She stopped to assess how many heavy sweaters and vests she had packed. "Aye, I think that should get me through."

Penny volunteered to drive Tessy to the airport and then have her or Jim pick her up upon her return home. Tommy had gladly offered to come over a couple of times a day to check on the animals. Tessy was feeling very blessed to have such wonderful friends and was able to go away without a care. Aye, things were working out the way they should. A good sign for sure, she thought.

The big day arrived and Penny was at Tessy's door in lots of time. They managed to hoist her luggage in the back of the SUV and they were off.

"I just want to thank ye again, Penny, for driving me all the way to Regina."

"Oh, no problem. I've been waiting to go in to the city to do some extreme shopping for some time now. This just gives me the perfect excuse." She laughed. "I should be thanking you."

"Oh, wonderful, and kind of ye to say. Sure glad the weather is cooperatin' for us."

"Yes. I really do not like driving on icy roads," Penny agreed. "I was talking to Dad last night. Sounds like the weather there has been good, too. Boy, is he excited to see you."

"Aye, and I him, to be sure. I am thinking, however, this will be the test of time," Tessy nervously chuckled.

"Oh, Tessy. You're not worried, are you?" Penny sounded concerned.

"Aye, maybe just a mite. 'Tis a big step we're taking."

"Yes, I know, but you two are so perfect for one another."

"Aye. I'm just havin' a few jitters, is all. Don't pay any mind to me."

"Tessy, let's wait until you get back and then we'll talk. Okay?"

"That's sounds like a wise idea, dear. Thank ye, kindly."

And with that, there was no more mention about any jitters. They hugged and kissed goodbye at the departure gate and Tessy was off to Winnipeg.

As the plane descended into her destination, Tessy peered out the window to see what she could recognize of the city she had left behind so many years ago. *My, has grown some, for sure,* she mused.

As Tessy made her way to the terminal exit, she noticed an elderly woman standing at the top of the escalator, glancing around looking a little confused as to where to go with people rushing past and bumping up against her. When Tessy reached her she put both her purse and carry-on in one hand, gently placed her free arm around the bewildered lady's shoulder, and said, "Hello, dear. I'm pretty sure we go this way. May I help you down the escalator?"

The elderly woman, with tears in her eyes, sighed with relief and nodded her head.

Tessy firmly took her arm and the two made their way safely down. They were half way down the escalator when Tessy spotted the most handsome, mischievous, grinning face standing out in the crowd. Her heart melted, quickened, and exploded with love as tears immediately sprang to her eyes. She was not expecting such an overwhelming reaction. When she reached the bottom, the woman's anxious relatives rushed over to collect her and thanked Tessy for her assistance. The little lady took both of Tessy's hands in hers, looked her square in the eyes, smiled and mouthed, "Thank you."

Marshall stood back until their tender moment was over and the family left; then he immediately took Tessy's bags and ushered her to the side. He dropped her bags, gathered her up in his arms and hugged and kissed her. He pulled away, looked down at her with his twinkling blue eyes and said, "What took ya so long?"

Tessy laughed and playfully slapped his chest. "Ye just never mind, ye cheeky rogue." And all her fears cleared and dissipated into thin air.

10
Best-Laid Plan

Dotty and Bert were at the door to greet Tessy when she arrived.

"Oh Tessy, how wonderful to see you. Congratulations! We couldn't be happier for the two of you," Dotty gushed as she reached for a hug.

"Thank ye, Dotty, grand to see you too. Aye, it is pretty exciting."

"Let me see that ring of yours. My… the good doctor does have excellent taste. Beautiful!" Dotty raved while holding Tessy's hand, admiring the precious gems.

"Aye. 'Tis lovely, I agree."

"Come in. Come in. Here, let me get your coat," offered Dotty. "Bert, maybe you should go out and help Dr. Tayse with the bags?"

"You bet. I was just on my way. Good to see you again, Tess. Congratulations," Bert added as he stepped past her and out the door.

After the bags were in and Tessy was settled, they all joined in the living room for drinks and appetizers.

Bert raised his glass. "Once again, congratulations you two. Cheers." They all raised their glasses and everyone took a drink in celebration.

"Thank you, Bert. As you both know, I couldn't be happier. And I'm hoping my bride-to-be feels the same," Marshall replied, gazing at his fiancée.

"Aye. Of course I am happy, love. We've just so many things to work out first. I've no idea where to start. 'Tis a little overwhelming, to be sure."

"Well, that's another reason I'm glad you're here, sweetheart, so we can work this out together. We are a team now, you know," Marshall said, raising his glass to her once again.

"Aye. I suppose we are. Sláinte." And they clinked glasses.

"Well, you will have ten wonderful days together to get at least some of it all figured out. Hopefully, you will soon pick a date and we can start with the arrangements. Have you decided where yet?" Dotty inquired.

"No. We don't even know that yet. But we will come to all of those decisions this week. Right Tessy?"

Tessy just smiled, raised her glass and took a drink.

The four of them spent an enjoyable evening together, including a meal fit for royalty. After everything was cleaned up, Dotty and Bert excused themselves to their guesthouse at the back of the property, so as to give Marshall and Tessy some private time. They went back into the living room to sit by the fire and just be together. There was an unusual awkwardness between them and they both knew the reason. Sleeping arrangements! It had not been discussed ahead of time as to just where Tessy's sleeping quarters would be. Dotty had Bert take her luggage up to the spare room, but Tessy was sure that was just for appearances so as not to embarrass her. Well, I guess this is the first thing we need to work out, ran through Tessy's mind. *No time like the present – Lord help a coward!*

They both started talking at the same time.

Marshall laughed. "Sorry, honey. Please go ahead."

"No, no. You first, love," Tessy insisted.

"Well, all right then. Instead of us both sitting here being uncomfortable, we should talk about where you would like to sleep while you're here. I know where I would like you to sleep, but I feel it's not up to me."

"Oh, Marshall. I just don't know. What about Dotty and Bert?"

"Well, honey. First off, they're old enough to understand what's going on. Second, it really is none of their business, and third, after tomorrow, I gave them a few days off so they could have some fun of their own which would also give us some alone time."

"Well, Marshall Tayse, ye certainly have thought of everything, to be sure. What am I goin' to do with ye?"

"Tessy, my lady, I do have a few suggestions," Marshall smirked, leaned down and kissed her.

Tessy had nothing left to do but gladly surrender.

She awoke the next morning snuggled close to Marshall with a faint grin on her face and a warm glow in her heart. She couldn't believe this was the way she was going to wake up every morning for the rest of her life. *I am so blessed and I do not take it for granted nor will I ever,* she told herself.

Marshall sensed her subtle movements and opened his eyes to gaze at her. "Good morning, my sweet lady of Ladyslipper." He leaned over and gently kissed her temple.

"Good mornin', love," Tessy smiled up at him.

Marshall cocked his head. "Speaking of which. I guess we should talk about whether you are going to continue to be the lady of Ladyslipper or the lady of Winnipeg?"

Tessy perched herself up on her elbows. "Great leaping leprechauns, man! Ye really like to get at things early in the day, don't ye? Let me wake up enough to get the cobwebs out of me head and a cup of coffee in me before ye start changin' the future."

"Whoa, whoa! Calm down, my Irish lass. I'm sorry, dear. I didn't mean to ruffle your feathers so early in the morning."

"Oh… sorry, love but my… ye must let me at least plant my feet on the floor before ye come up with questions such as that. Aye, these are things that need discussin' but I wasn't expectin' ye to jump right in with it before I've even got my eyes fully opened!"

"Okay, sweetheart. I'll let you have your coffee from now on before I start with any life changing suggestions. Either that or I'm going to have to learn how to duck a lot quicker to stay out of the way of that Irish dander of yours." He laughed and pulled her down to him and playfully squeezed her.

"Aye. That's the best laid plan ye've had so far today!" Tessy muffled from her buried position.

By the time Tessy made her way to the kitchen, Marshall had a cup of coffee in each hand. When he saw her, he immediately stretched one of the cups out toward her and playfully ducked.

Tessy laughed wholeheartedly! She took the offering. Marshall laughed too, put his arm around her shoulders, leaned down for a kiss, and said, "Sure glad we can joke and laugh along this journey we're planning. It's certainly going to make it a lot more enjoyable."

"Aye. But what am I to do with ye? I never know what you're up to next."

"Yes. And I plan to keep it that way. So hang on, my lady!"

"Aye. I'm afraid it's going to be quite a ride, love." She laughed again, raised her cup to his, then took a drink.

11
Relief, Rapture and Arrangements

After a leisurely breakfast and a visit with Dotty and Bert, Tessy and Marshall decided to go for a long walk and get some fresh air. As they sauntered along, hand in hand, they easily chatted about the kids, work and life in general. Marshall was becoming sadly aware that they were discussing everything but what they should be… the wedding!

"Tessy? Is there something bothering you?" he blurted.

"Bothering me? What do ye mean, love?"

"Well, you really haven't mentioned the wedding all morning, and you seem a little distant. You haven't changed your mind about marrying me, have you?"

Tessy halted and looked up at the wounded man. "Oh Marshall! No, of course not. I'm so sorry if I've given ye that notion, dear." She wrapped her arms around his middle and gave him a reassuring hug.

"Boy, that's a relief!" Marshall sighed and hugged her back.

They stood for a moment in silence just holding one another. Tessy lifted her head and reluctantly said, "However, there is something that has been gnawing at me that I would like to get off my shoulders, if ye don't mind."

There was a bench just down the way so Marshall grabbed her hand and said, "Of course, sweetheart. Let's go sit down and you can tell me whatever it is that's on your mind."

Once seated, Tessy looked up at him and nervously smiled. "I'm not really sure how to say this as I am worried it may offend ye."

"Tessy. I think we are a little past that, at this point. You can tell me anything,"

"Well, I don't want to hurt ye, then."

"Tessy McGuigan! What are you getting at?"

"Actually, Tessy McGuigan, is what I'm getting at."

"Sweetheart, you're talking in riddles."

"Oh Marshall. It's just that I've been Tessy McGuigan the majority of my life and I'm not quite sure that I'm ready to change my name to something else."

Marshall started to laugh. "Oh, sweetheart! Is that what you've been so upset about since you've been here? Changing your name! I fell in love with you, not your name. It could be Rumplestiltskin for all I care. I would never ask you to change your name if you didn't want to."

Tessy was so relieved she started to cry. She hadn't wanted to hurt Marshall, yet she needed to be true to herself. Marshall wrapped her in his arms and let her cry it out. Once she collected herself, she took his face in her hands, gently kissed him and said, "You are such an amazing man. Again, I feel like the most blessed woman on the face of this beautiful earth. You have no idea what a weight you have lifted from me."

Marshall kissed the tip of her nose. "Now, can we start planning a wedding?"

"Most definitely! Oh Marshall… I have some enchanting ideas!"

Marshall just laughed.

They rushed home, made some hot chocolate, pulled out a calendar, got a pen and paper, and set right to work at the dining room table. By lunch they had narrowed down a date and decided that a simple garden wedding would be perfect, especially since booking a venue now would be next to impossible with the big day only a few months away.

Now, the big question… whose garden… Tessy's or Marshall's? Tessy had the largest, most lush yard and gardens, but Ladyslipper would mean highway travelling for some. Marshall's yard was smaller yet very nice and, of course, Tessy would have no problem creating a magically elegant garden setting. Winnipeg also had the airport, making for easy travel arrangements. Dotty called them to the kitchen for lunch. They decided they would work on the guest list after they ate, and maybe that would help make the decision.

Dotty had a steaming bowl of homemade tomato bisque and a chicken Caesar salad wrap laid out on the table for them.

"Oh, Dotty, dear. This looks wonderful. Thank ye for takin' such good care of us," Tessy commented as Marshall pulled out her chair for her.

"You're very welcome, Tessy. I enjoy preparing meals and fussing over people. Especially when they appreciate it."

"Fussing over people is putting it mildly, I'd say!" Marshall looked over at her and chuckled.

Tessy came to Dotty's defense. "Now, Marshall Tayse. Ye just never mind about teasing this wonderful angel that watches over ye."

"I know. Just kidding. I don't know where I'd be without Dotty or Bert."

"Aye. And it's good thing ye know that, too."

"Well, thank you both. We love being here. It's been our home for a lot of years, now."

After lunch they were soon back at it, and they tenaciously worked all afternoon on the guest list. They couldn't believe the time, when Dotty came in and announced there were some appetizers ready and waiting in the living room. They decided to call it a day, left all the papers right where they lay, and retired to the living room for some well deserved refreshments and a contented, relaxing evening.

"Well, how are the arrangements coming along, you two?" Dotty asked as she was serving Tessy some shrimp dip to go with her cracker.

"Oh, Dotty, they are coming about just grand. I couldn't be more excited!" Tessy raved.

"That's great! It's nice to see you so happy. If you don't mind me saying, you just haven't quite seemed yourself, up until now," Dotty smiled at her.

"Well… thanks to our good doctor, here, all my fears have been released and I am now enraptured in nothing but happiness."

Everyone, including Tessy herself, laughed at her degree of enthusiasm.

"Soooo… may I ask if you've decided on a date yet?" Dotty cautiously asked.

"Yes! I am very happy to say we have finally picked a day." Marshall raised his glass towards Tessy. "Honey, will you do the honours of making the big announcement?"

Tessy smiled with a slight blush. "We have decided on the second weekend in June. That way we have almost a week to tidy things up before we leave for our trip to Ireland."

"Which will be the honeymoon of the century!" Marshall spouted.

"Well, we've lots to do before then, love. And, I can't wait to get up and start on plans again tomorrow morning."

"Whoa… …hold on there, my little Irish lass. Not tomorrow. Tomorrow is a very special day, is it not? Like someone's birthday, perhaps?" Marshall reached his long arm around her and gently rubbed her shoulder. "I have a few things planned for you."

"Oh now, go on with ye. There's no need to be doin' anything fancy tomorrow. I certainly don't need any shenanigans of any kind."

To which Marshall replied, "Well, my lady of Ladyslipper, you let me worry about that," as he leaned over for a kiss.

12
Celebrate in Style

It was early when Tessy awoke to find Marshall staring and smiling at her. "Good morning, sweetheart. Happy Birthday."

"Good mornin'. Thank ye," she chuckled, rubbing the sleep from her eyes and trying to fluff her flattened, slept on hair.

"Well, I have a few things to do this morning so why don't you spoil yourself and go back to sleep for a while? It's still pretty early."

"Is there anything I can help ye with?"

"No. But thank you. Go back to sleep, dear." Marshall kissed her forehead and got out of bed.

"Aye. Thank ye, love. I might just do that," Tessy sleepily mumbled as she snuggled deeper under the comforter.

A little over an hour later she yawned and stretched herself awake. She lay quietly for a few moments enjoying her feelings of being refreshed, happy and grateful. "Well, thank ye, Lord, for gracing me with a life greater than what I could have ever hoped for. Here I am, another year older, and you just keep bestowing such amazing blessings upon me. I pray that you continue to guide me in paying it forward in any way I can. Have a good day, Lord. I'm sure I'm in store for one!" And with that she threw back the covers and firmly plunked her grateful feet on the floor.

Downstairs, she found Dotty alone in the kitchen setting out some pastries on a lovely platter.

"Good mornin' to ye, Dotty, dear," Tessy chirped.

Startled, Dotty swung around. "Oh, good morning, Tessy. I didn't hear you come in. Happy birthday. Did you sleep well?"

"Thank ye. Aye, I did. Even caught a few extra winks this morning," she chuckled.

"Well, that's good. You'll probably need it. I think Dr. Tayse is going to keep you rather busy today, from what I understand. Oh, I hope I haven't spoiled anything for you," she gasped.

Tessy just laughed. "Dotty dear, I don't think you're telling me anything that I haven't already figured out with that scalawag."

Dotty chuckled. "Yes, I guess you're right. Can I get you a coffee? And here, try one of these. I had one a little earlier. They are amazing. Dr. Tayse brought them back fresh from the bakery this morning, already."

"Aye. Thank you, Dotty. My, they do look delicious. Maybe just one wouldn't hurt. Where is that scamp, anyway?"

"Oh, he and Bert are out running some errands before Bert and I take off for a few days."

"Really," Tessy suspiciously commented as she took another bite of her pastry.

As the two women cleaned up the kitchen they chatted about the wedding arrangements.

"So, are you two any closer to picking which location you think might suit you best?" Dotty asked as she wiped the counter.

"To be perfectly honest, it is beginning to look like Ladyslipper, believe it or not. It seems my guest list is a little longer than his. Marshall said that other than family, including you and Bert, there weren't very many people he would ask. He said that after Evelyne passed, he sort of drifted away from their friends, and that left maybe a few colleagues to invite."

"I suppose that's true. Our good doctor hasn't socialized much." Dotty turned quiet and continued on with her cleaning.

Tessy sensed something was not quite right. "Dotty, what is it?"

"It's not my place to say," was her reply.

"Dotty, dear. Please tell me what's bothering ye."

"Well, it's just that I was so looking forward to helping with all the preparations and… well… fussing, like I do, over you and Dr. Tayse." She now sounded a little embarrassed.

Tessy laughed. "Dotty! We would never leave ye out. Of course ye'll be included in the preparations. You and Bert can come and stay with me at Ashling Manor for the weeks coming up to the wedding. Marshall will probably be there as well, and we can all spend our days getting everything ready."

"Oh Tessy! That would be wonderful. Do you really think we could?"

"Of course. It would be lovely to have ye there. And we'll be glad of the help, for sure!"

The two women hugged and all wounded feelings were considered patched.

A while later, Marshall and Bert returned. Tessy went to the door to greet them when Bert intercepted and took Tessy back into the kitchen. "Happy birthday, Tessy. Will you join me for a celebratory cup of coffee?"

"Bert Mitchell! Ye're not fooling anyone by being as subtle as a train wreck! What on earth is that man up to?"

"Why, Tessy. I'm crushed! I have no idea what you're talking about," Bert smirked.

"Aye. I'm sure," Tessy scolded him.

Just then, Marshall came calmly walking around the corner. "What's up all? Oh, Tessy. You're up. Did you sleep well, dear?"

"Don't be dearing me, Dr. Tayse. What is it that you've been up to for the past two hours? And then come in here sneaking around like a naughty fox."

"Tess… I didn't know you had such a suspicious nature. Apparently, we have lots of things yet to find out about one another. Coffee, anyone?" he said as he held up the coffee pot with great flair in one hand and grabbed a pastry with the other.

"You're not fooling me one bit and don't be thinkin' that ye are."

Everyone laughed, filled their cups and enjoyed the rest of their coffee together as Dotty and Bert were soon leaving for their mini-holiday.

"So, Dotty, Bert, where are ye off to for your little get-a-way?"

Bert smiled and picked up Dotty's hand, "We're off to a beautiful resort at Riding Mountain National Park – well, just outside the park, actually. We've rented a one-bedroom chalet and we are going to enjoy some outdoor activities and just relax."

"Sounds grand!" Tessy clapped her hands. "I've been to Riding Mountain, but it has been a long while and only in the summer months. I'd love to see it in the winter."

"Well, darling, we'll have to put that on our bucket list." Marshall put his arm around her.

They soon finished up, and Bert was hauling suitcases out to the car.

"Now Tessy, I've fixed you and Dr. Tayse a bite of lunch and popped it in the refrigerator. There should be enough groceries, and I made sure I left plenty of baking as you know how the good doctor loves his sweets," Dotty fussed as she was headed out the door.

"Oh, Dotty, dear. Thank ye so much, but ye shouldn't have troubled yourself. Marshall and I will be just fine. Ye just go and have a wonderful time. See you in a few days." Tessy reached for a hug, and she and Marshall waved them off down the driveway. They were headed down the hallway to the kitchen when the phone rang. Marshall answered it and a strange look came over him as he handed the phone to Tessy. She gingerly took it.

"Aye, it is. Oh, Cache, dear, what is it? Has something happened? Oh, my! Oh no. No, no, no. He was doing me a grand favour watching my house and animals for me. He's a fine decent lad. No, no charges at all. I'll be home in about a week and can come down and sign whatever it is ye need. I will properly apologize to him then. And Cache, thank ye for calling and straightening this all out before it got out of hand. Bye, for now, dear."

Marshall couldn't wait for the explanation!

"That was Cherokee's father, Cache. I believe I've mentioned to ye, he is a constable in Ladyslipper. Well, it seems that Mrs. Chamberlain saw Tommy entering my house when he came over to feed the animals, called the police and had him arrested. Poor Tommy. What a thing to happen to ye when you're just doing a good deed. I'll have to make it up to him when I get home. My, that Mrs. Chamberlain is quite a prize! Can't keep her nose out of anything, although maybe she thought she was helping. Oh well, what's done is done."

"Well, if you ask me, I'd say Mrs. Chamberlain is the booby-prize!" Marshall chuckled, shaking his head, as they set the table for lunch.

Marshall and Tessy were just finishing up an early lunch when he suggested that they go down to The Forks and skate along the river for the afternoon.

"Oh, Marshall. That sounds lovely but I didn't bring my skates. There's not much room to pack such apparel when you're flying," she laughed.

"Not a problem, my lady. I remembered when we went skating on New Year's Eve you said your skates were pretty old and you wanted to get new ones, so… I thought we'd go down to the sports store on our way and get you a new pair. Part of my birthday gift to you."

"Marshall, that's not necessary. I can buy my own skates."

"Of course you can. But as I said, they will be part of your birthday gift. I insist."

"Aye. Ye are a stubborn man, Dr. Tayse."

"Thank you," Marshall said as he bowed his head. "Do you have enough warm clothes with you, dear?"

"Aye. That I do and ye'll not be insisting that ye buy me a new wardrobe or ye'll have the fight of your life on your hands," Tessy threatened.

"Wouldn't dream of it, my lady."

Before long they were gracefully gliding down the frozen Assiniboine River, taking in all the sights and activities. There were dozens of unique warming huts staggered all along the way, and they stopped at most of them just to take a look. Even with hundreds of other people enjoying the afternoon, it never felt crowded and their time together remained intimately special. They were resting in one of the huts when Marshall looked at his watch and said, "Oh honey, we have to get going."

Tessy looked up at him rather puzzled.

Marshall laughed, grabbed her hand and pulled her up on to her skates. "I'll explain on the way," he assured.

They removed their skates, returned to the car, and Marshall announced that he had booked her a surprise spa for the remaining of the afternoon.

"Oh Marshall! Thank ye but I don't need such pampering as that," Tessy responded; however, she was unable to contain a glittering smile of excitement.

"Well, you spend most of your time pampering and looking after everyone else, so I thought it was high time someone did that for you." He pulled up to the entrance, got out, opened her door and took her hand. "I'll pick you up in a few hours. You enjoy yourself." He leaned over and kissed her.

For the rest of the afternoon Tessy truly believed she had reached heaven. All the products were natural and organic, while the lovely ladies that worked their magic on her were sweet, professional and amazing. Tessy had never been so pampered. *What was it I did to charm such a man as Marshall Tayse?* she wondered as she lay back with cool fresh cucumber slices gently placed over her eyes, a strawberry mask lathered on her face, and what surely must have been an angel massaging her feet.

Three hours after Marshall dropped her off, she floated back out to the entrance area where he was patiently waiting for her. He took one look at her and burst out laughing. "Well darling, you certainly do look relaxed!"

All Tessy could sigh, right at that moment, was "Aye. It was heaven," and she laid her head into his chest.

"Don't fade on me just yet, sweetheart. We have a birthday dinner to get you through first. We have reservations at the Fort Gary Hotel in two hours."

"Oh Marshall!"

"Well, we had such a romantic evening there the last time you were here I thought maybe you'd like to repeat it, and possibly even improve on it considering we are completely alone this time."

Tessy smiled up at him, winked and stretched on her tiptoes for a kiss.

Back at the house they enjoyed a cocktail after they had dressed for the evening. They were waiting for the limousine Marshall had rented for the evening. He mentioned to Tessy he had also requested Colin, the same driver who had ushered them around during her visit at Thanksgiving.

"Aye. I remember him well. A fine young lad."

"Well, he should be here any minute, my lady."

"Aye. I should just pop off to freshen up then, love."

"No rush, sweetheart. We've got the entire evening to ourselves."

Colin soon arrived and their enchanting evening began. There was no rushing; the evening was theirs and they filled every moment with enjoyment, laughter and love. It was truly a day that had been celebrated in style!

13
Festive Fun and Fancy

Tessy awoke with a start, not realizing where she was at first. Then she felt Marshall snuggled close to her back and his arm gently draped over her waist. She let out a deep sigh of contentment, which woke Marshall.

"Sorry, love. I didn't mean to wake ye."

"Every waking moment with you is a pleasure, my lady," was his comeback. Then he nestled into the back of her neck, kissing and tickling her. Giggling, she scrunched up her neck and turned toward him, putting her arms around his neck. "Thank ye so much for a wonderful birthday. I don't think I've ever enjoyed one as much. There isn't anything more I could have wished for."

"Well, I have one more thing for you," he answered as he reached over to the nightstand, opened the drawer and pulled out a small box.

"Marshall Tayse! Was yesterday not enough?"

"Not for you." He smiled and kissed her.

She took the box and slowly opened it to reveal a gorgeous emerald bracelet.

"Oh Marshall! It's beautiful," she whispered.

He threw her a cocky smirk. "It finally arrived yesterday morning, so Bert and I went to pick it up while you were still sleeping – or you were supposed to be! I would have given it to you last night but when we got home it was very late and we had other things on our mind… soooo… quite frankly, I actually forgot all about it."

Tessy's return smirk was perhaps what a person might call more impish before she passionately kissed him.

They spent the next couple of days just enjoying their alone time and continuing on with their wedding plans. Due to the finalization of the guest list, the decision to have the wedding in Ladyslipper was confirmed. So, for now, that was about all they could accomplish regarding the nuptials.

The day before Valentine's, Marshall surprised Tessy by suggesting that they just stay home for Valentine's dinner and cook up some lobster.

"Marshall Tayse! Ye never cease to keep me guessin'. What a wonderful way to spend such a romantic evening. And, oh my, you won't have to ask me twice about a lobster dinner!"

Marshall laughed. "Great. Then we'll get up tomorrow morning, do some shopping, and go and pick out a beauty."

"Oh, about that… I just can't do it. I'm afraid you'll have to go and pick out the poor little soul by yourself. And I don't want to be anywhere near the kitchen at that terrible moment. I sure wish there was some other way to prepare lobster. It is so delicious. I don't suppose ye'd consider frozen?"

Again, Marshall laughed. "Well, honey, fresh is much better. However, if you're going to hide out in the other room all evening, maybe we should. We'll make that call tomorrow."

Valentine's day, Marshall had a dozen red roses delivered for his lady, and Tessy surprised him with a beautiful Celtic pocket watch, very much like the one she had given Jim for Christmas. Marshall impressed Tessy by taking her to his favourite Irish pub, The Olde Emerald Stone, for a lovely bite of pub-fare along with a Guinness, then for a stroll along the river. Before they went home they stopped and made their lobster call, which in the end turned out to be crab legs, and continued on to the house.

The magical evening was filled with music to dance to, fabulous food, fine wine and memorable romance.

Marshall had pre-purchased tickets for the Festival du Voyageur, so the next day was spent outside in joyous fun. They caught an early shuttle down to Voyageur Park in Saint-Boniface and entered the gate just in time to watch some children shooting down the toboggan ramp screaming with delight, which made both Marshall and Tessy give out a heartfelt belly laugh. They wandered around admiring the massive ice sculptures designed by artists from all over the world, trying to decide which one was their favourite. Marshall was still engrossed in the sculptures when Tessy spied where people were making maple syrup candy in the snow, and she couldn't resist. She watched them pour a long bead of syrup down the ice counter, then take a wooden stick and twist the sweet strip around and around it, and hand the treat to her. She paid and thanked the young girl. Marshall snuck up behind her, called "Caught 'cha!" and wrapped his arms around her.

Tessy laughed and raised the candy up for him to sample.

"Man, you can't beat that. I'll be getting one of those for me as soon as we finish lunch."

The snowshoe races were about to commence, so they thought they'd head over and get a good spot. Some of the contestants were amazingly good at maneuvering the snowshoes at quite a speed, while others got their feet tangled and ended up stumbling. All in all it was very entertaining.

They soon were back to wandering and found themselves in the gift shop. Marshall picked up a traditional, brightly woven, voyageur sash with the long fringe.

"I've always wanted one of these," he mentioned to Tessy who was standing nearby.

"Well then, love, there's no time like the present. If ye've always pined for one then you should have one."

"What the heck… why not? Why don't you get one, too?"

"Aye. That would be fun. However, I think I'll be wearin' mine around my neck, not my waist." They both walked back out into the sunny, cold day, feeling as festive as they looked wearing their new purchases.

For the rest of the day, they ate traditional cuisine, listened to traditional music, and watched traditional dance while enjoying all the sights and sounds of this amazing event. It was late afternoon and they were in the ice hut, which was serving the Festival's famous wine, Caribou.

"Boy, I sure wish we could get this other times of the year," Marshall said as he held up his glass made of ice.

"Aye. It is too bad that it is only at the Festival you can get it. But my, what a feather in their cap this lovely wine is."

They went to warm up and enjoy some of the special entertainment in the main tent before bundling up and heading out to the shuttle which would take them back to their car.

"Oh Marshall… again, what a wonderful day. Thank ye so much, love," Tessy mused out loud on their way, hand in hand.

"It was fun. Wasn't it?" Marshall smiled down at her as he fussed with her new scarf.

Their trip home was rather quiet, but very comfortable. It had been a long, enjoyable day.

14
A Timeworn Question Resolved

The majority of the next day Marshall was going to be busy. He had to go in to the office for a while as well as make his rounds at the hospital. They decided this it would be a great time for Tessy to go and visit her godmother, Aunt Shannon. Arrangements were made and Marshall dropped her off early in the day.

After Tessy's parents had been killed in a car accident over in Ireland, she and Keenan had been sent to Winnipeg to live with their godmother, Aunt Shannon, and her family. They had become very close, and Tessy was looking forward to a wonderful visit. As soon as she walked in, she noticed that Aunt Shannon was not looking as spry as usual.

"Hello, Auntie Shannon. Come, let's sit and have a fine visit."

"Hello, Tessy, dear. Aye. That would be grand." And the two ladies hugged and headed for the front room and sat down.

"I've made us a nice pot of tea. It's in the kitchen. I'll just go fetch it," Aunt Shannon started to get up.

"No, no, Auntie. I'll go. You sit. I remember where everything is."

When Tessy returned, she set the tea on the coffee table and sat down beside her aunt on the couch. She had never seen her aunt look so tiny and frail and it worried her. "Auntie, are you all right? Are you feeling well?"

"Aye, dear. Just a wee weary, is all." Aunt Shannon smiled up at her and patted her hand.

Tessy blinked away a tear as she busied herself with pouring the tea.

"So ye're plannin' a weddin', are ye? How wonderful."

"Aye, 'tis a pretty exciting time, to be sure." Tessy smiled as she handed her a cup.

"Well, ye couldn't have found yourself a better lad than the one I met at Thanksgiving."

"Aye, Auntie. I agree."

They had a wonderful visit catching up on the latest news and spending time reminiscing over days gone past. Tessy could see that her aunt was tiring and suggested that while she make some lunch, Aunt Shannon should rest on the day-bed for a bit. It didn't take a great deal of persuasion.

Rummaging around in Aunt Shannon's kitchen brought back so many memories. Tessy chuckled. Even though there had been a few updates over the years, everything was pretty much in the same place as when she lived here. When the soup was hot and the sandwiches were made, Tessy peeked in the other room to see if she was awake yet. Not yet. Well, that's just fine, I'll go fetch the photo albums and have a go at them. She had methodically thumbed through them for quite a while when she thought she heard some rustling in the front room.

"Auntie, how are ye feeling? Can I help ye up, dear?"

"Aye. That 'twould be grand. Not quite as limber as I used to be."

Tessy helped her to her feet and let her freshen up while she went back to kitchen to reheat and dish up the soup.

"That looks lovely, dear. Thank ye kindly," Aunt Shannon remarked as she made her way over to the table. As they ate, Shannon spied the albums Tessy had been probing.

"Wonderful memories, those," she sighed as she motioned with her elbow.

"Aye. I was having a grand time going through them. I don't recognize some of the people in the old ones from Ireland. May we spend some time going over them after lunch to see if you can help me with that?"

"Aye, of course, dear. My kids, or your uncle Steven for that matter, never had much love for the old country. I guess, considering they weren't from there, they wouldn't have had much use for it. I was hopin' that would change when we went over to visit but it didn't. It was truly a blessin' when ye and Keenan came to live with us. Made me feel like I wasn't so alone in this new country."

"Oh Auntie! I had no idea that was the way ye were feelin' back then."

"Of course not, dear. Ye two were devastated when ye got here and it took some time for the pair of ye to settle in. I wasn't about to leave my troubles on your doorstep, too."

"Auntie, you were just as devastated as we were, losing your only sister, but ye took us in and raised us like your own. For that, Keenan and I will be forever grateful."

They finished up and headed back into the front room with the albums and a cup of tea. They were sitting close with the shared album opened up on their laps. Before they got started, Shannon looked up at Tessy and confided, "Tessy, love. It's going to be my time soon, and I need to share something with ye before that happens."

Tessy started to rebut this particular conversation.

"Tessy! Listen to what an old woman has to say!" Aunt Shannon barked. Tessy knew better than to argue with that tone of voice and remained silent.

"I know you and Keenan always wondered why it was me that your folks chose for your guardian, and I never gave ye a straight answer. Well, I am now." She looked down into her lap and hesitated. "Your mam and I come from a long line of *the gifted* and she knew that the two of ye had the gift. I know ye feel it in your soul from time to time, and Keenan, too, if he'd just give in and stop fightin' it. She was hopin' if ye came to live with me you'd not lose it. The good Lord knows, I tried to keep it up, but with a house full of nonbelievers it was a losin' battle. I just hope she forgives me." Shannon put her hands over her face and began to weep.

Tessy pulled Shannon into her arms and rocked her back and forth. "Oh, Auntie, there's nothing to forgive. You were wonderful to us and we could not have been raised by anyone who loved us more and gave us everything we could have wished for. Mam couldn't have wished for anything more, as well. She knew where we needed to be and watched over us every step of the way. Aye, I do know I carry the gift and I have great respect for it. It was you that helped me continue on with my love of gardenin' and herbs, and to instill that into a sixteen year old… well… there had to be some magick in there somewhere! So, see… ye did a fine job." She smiled at her and gave her a kiss on the cheek.

"Thank ye, dear, so kind of ye to say. Just tellin' ye has taken such a load off my weary shoulders." She smiled back at Tessy and patted her hand. "Ye do still have that wee package from your mam I gave ye on Thanksgiving? That is one promise to her that I never gave up on."

"Aye, Auntie. It's in a safe place and I will open it as you instructed me to do so."

"Grand, thank ye. I've sent one to Keenan, as well, with the same instructions. Neither of ye are to open them until I'm in the ground and the two of ye are alone together."

"Aye. He and I have agreed."

"Grand. Grand. Now, I'd like ye to take these old photo albums with ye after we look through them one more time. I know my kids have no use for these old ones from Ireland, and I know that you and Keenan will have much enjoyment looking over them. Especially the pictures of your mam and me when we were wee tykes."

"Oh Auntie! I would love to have them, but are you sure you are ready for me to take them now?"

"Aye. It's time they went home."

They spent the rest of the afternoon going over pictures, laughing, remembering, and being grateful for their shared loving bond and unique heritage. Tessy was very careful to write down the names of the people she didn't know or whom she had questions about. She wasn't sure why but she felt it to be quite important.

Tessy called Marshall and asked if he could pick up some take-out and join them for supper there. She was not ready to say her good-byes just yet – she wanted today to last as long as possible. Auntie Shannon had definitely gone downhill and Tessy could see her light fading. She felt she was losing something – someone so very special, and life would never be the same again.

15

A Bittersweet Day

On their way home from Aunt Shannon's, they mostly chatted about Marshall's day while Tessy held tight to the treasured photo albums. Marshall instinctively understood their value and did not even ask to carry them for her.

When they reached the house, the lights were on which meant Dotty and Bert had made it home. Marshall opened the door and ushered Tessy in. Dotty trotted down the hall to greet them.

"Hello. Hello." Tessy gathered her up and gave her a hug. "How was your wee holiday?"

"Oh, Tessy! It was amazing! Hello, Dr. Tayse," Dotty returned. "Where were you two off to?"

"I went and spent the day with Aunt Shannon. We had a marvelous visit."

"Wonderful. How is she doing?"

"Well, not as good as I hoped. But she is still as feisty as ever," Tessy chuckled.

"Glad to hear she's putting up a good fight. She is such a fine lady."

Soon they were all seated in the living room enjoying a glass of wine. They each shared their own detailed accounts of what had gone on for the past few days. Tessy was glad that they could focus on the positive that had happened this week, as it eased the cloud of concern she was feeling over Aunt Shannon.

The next morning, Tessy's first thought was that this was her last full day here. Where had the days gone? She stretched and let out a content sigh, then rolled over and snuggled into Marshall's back.

She was sure going to miss this but she was looking forward to getting back home. It had been long enough.

When they made their way downstairs to the kitchen, Dotty was in the process of making them a traditional Irish breakfast. Tessy laughed when she realized what she was doing.

"Now, Dotty, dear, what are ye up to?"

"Well, top-o-the-mornin' to ye! I just thought I'd get you ready and thinking about that wonderful honeymoon you two are going to be on in just a few short months."

"Oh, Dotty, thank ye kindly. What a thoughtful thing to do. And, my, it does smell delicious!"

Marshall and Tessy sat down to eggs, bangers, potato wedges, fried mushrooms, fried tomatoes and toast.

"Sorry, Tessy, just couldn't do the blood sausage," Dotty scrunched up her face.

"Not to worry, dear. I don't miss it a lick. This couldn't be any better than if it was prepared in me own mam's kitchen."

"That goes for me, too. I, for sure, don't miss it!" Marshall piped. Tessy laughed.

They were sitting enjoying a cup of coffee when Marshall asked Tessy what she would like to do for her last day.

"Hmmm… " Tessy glanced up into the air, "I've been hearing some wonderful things about the new Canadian Museum for Human Rights. Have you been yet?"

"No. But I've been wanting to. Every time I drive by that magnificent building I think I really ought to do that. So, is that our plan for today?"

"Aye, that would be grand. Not to mention, we need to walk off some of this breakfast."

"Well, the Canadian Museum for Human Rights, it is then." Marshall slapped his knee.

They spent three hours just wandering around the museum taking in all the history and knowledge available to them. Tessy understood why the museum stated it was an Exhibit About Love and Forgiveness. She found it heart wrenching, informative, inspirational and encouraging. She felt spiritually stimulated in the presence of such antiquity. To her, it was reverent and she felt honoured to be privy to it.

When they were satisfied with their museum tour they decided to go back to the Conservatory, which they had also visited during her Thanksgiving stay. Tessy never tired of those surroundings, the gorgeous plants, the humidity, the smells, the lushness and the sounds of the water fountain. It was beautiful. She was enjoying it immensely; however, she sensed quite a different aura around Marshall. He was feeling bittersweet about Tessy leaving in less than twenty-four hours and he was not hiding it well.

"Marshall, love. What is it?" Tessy hugged his arm.

"You're leaving tomorrow and I am going to miss you so much. This has just been wonderful having you here with me every day."

"Marshall, we've been through this before and we will manage it again. Please try and stay positive about our living arrangements. It is what it is and must be for now. I'm going to miss you, too," and she hugged his arm again.

"All right… I'll stop pouting." He sheepishly grinned down at her.

Tessy laughed. "Good." She pulled him behind a lush bush and gave him a kiss, then playfully scooted away for him to chase her.

It was late afternoon when they returned home, and Dotty had refreshments set up in the living room for just the two of them. They spent their last night together in a romantic haze. Dotty had prepared a beautiful prime rib and Yorkshire pudding dinner with all the fixings. The two of them sat in the dining room with only candles for lighting and soft music playing. They celebrated a dozen toasts to one another over intimate conversation and affectionate gazes. After supper they slow danced and held each other close. They retired early and spent one last night embraced in love.

Tessy's flight was booked for late morning, so the Tayse residence was a hubbub of activity early in the day. Tessy was busy packing, Dotty was preparing breakfast, and Marshall was pacing. Bert was having coffee.

"You could be doing something, Bert!" Dotty huffed at him in exasperation.

"Like what? There's enough going on around here without me getting in the way. I'll go and warm up the SUV in a little while. It's a bit too early yet."

"Oh, I guess you're right. It's just that we're going to miss her so much, especially the good doctor. I wish something could be done about this," Dotty said, shaking her head.

"Honey, stop fretting. There's nothing we can do, and it just makes it harder on everyone, you included."

"Oh, I know," she sighed.

Two hours later, after a tearful good-bye between Tessy and Dotty, Marshall and Tessy were on their way to the airport. They made small talk so the silence would not become deafening. Marshall groaned as the airport came into view.

"Now, Marshall Tayse, we are not going to make this a long, drawn out good-bye. We'll be seeing one another very soon, I'm sure, so let's just do this and get it over with. I've had a marvelous holiday and I thank you so much for all the wonderful places and things we've seen."

"You're right, sweetheart. Okay. I'll just take your bags in and get you settled and maybe just hang out with you for a while until it's time for you to go through the departure gates."

They got her bags checked and went for a coffee. It really didn't seem as bad as what Marshall thought it was going to. Tessy seemed to put a calmness in him. When it was time, he walked her to the departures gate. They hugged, kissed, and Tessy waved good-bye while she was in the line-up until he was out of sight. *I am going to miss him, yet I am so looking forward to returning home*, was Tessy's thought as she wiped away the tear that trickled down her cheek.

16
A Guest for Ashling Manor

Penny was waiting for Tessy when she arrived. They chatted nonstop all the way back to Ladyslipper. Penny was quite relieved to hear that Tessy and her father had had a marvelous time and that some wedding arrangements had been made. She was very excited that they were going to be married in Ladyslipper. She couldn't wait to get home and share the good news. The kids would be ecstatic.

Before they knew it, they were turning into Tessy's lane. Oh, what a welcome sight Ashling Manor was! As good a time as she'd had, Tessy was so looking forward to her home and quiet little life. She'd never taken it for granted but now was even more grateful for it. She thanked Penny for meeting her, while trying to give her some money for gas, but again, Penny said she had to go to the city anyway so there was no need. However, she eagerly accepted the gifts of maple syrup and candy. Tessy got some of her luggage out of the back and made her way up the steps to unlock the door. She could hear the dogs making a fuss on the other side and was just as anxious to see them. Once the door opened, the dogs came thundering out to greet her, tails wagging, tongues out and paws up-stretched for attention. What a wonderful greeting, Tessy thought as she rubbed and hugged while making a fuss with cooing loving messages for them. A few moments later, she realized Penny was trying to lug the rest of her suitcases out of the car and ran down to help out.

"Sorry, dear. I was just lost with my pups for a moment. Here let me get that."

Between the two of them they got everything into the house and Tessy somewhat settled.

"Would ye like to come in for a tea, Penny? It would take but a minute to get the kettle on."

"Oh, thanks, Tessy but no. The kids get out of school early today so I'd like to be home when they get there."

"Aye. I understand, dear. Another time, then. Thank you, again, for coming to rescue me and gettin' me home safe and sound."

"No problem, Tessy. See you soon."

"Aye. Bye, bye now." Tessy reached for a hug, then stood at the door and waved good-bye until Penny was down the lane. She closed the door and smiled as she turned to look around her familiar surroundings. Oh, my Ashling Manor… how I missed you. Always standing so sturdy and true. Welcoming me with open arms, gentle spirit and loving memories… soon new memories to be made.

Before she even started to unpack, she decided she had better give Marshall a quick call to let him know she'd arrived just fine. Marshall was relieved to hear from her, and they chatted for a few minutes. When she hung up she had mixed emotions. She did miss him terribly, but she was so very happy to be home.

Tessy walked over to the thermostat and cranked it up before carrying her bags up to her room to start putting things away with the dogs not far from her. The cats, on the other hand, were giving her the cold shoulder for leaving them for so long, and worse yet, leaving them in the house for ten days with only the dogs! She realized they would continue with their little charade for a couple of days before they would show any affection. Tessy chuckled at their personalities. "Which reminds me," she blurted out loud to Duke, who was lying on her floor mat by the bed. "I must go downtown tomorrow and pick up a gift certificate for Tommy for looking after you rascals. That, and his troubles because of Mrs. Chamberlain. Aye, I must not forget to do that straight off."

Tessy had carefully unpacked the photo albums Aunt Shannon insisted she take home. When everything else was put away, she took them downstairs and placed them on the side table by the big chair in the library. She needed to leave them out for easy access, for some reason.

It wasn't long and she was all settled in. The house was warming up nicely but she decided to go into the living room and start a lovely fire. After she had it roaring, she closed the screen and headed to the kitchen to pull out the rest of the frozen stew left over from her evening with Tommy. That made her think to give the Bakers a call and let them know she was home and that Tommy wouldn't need to come over and check on the animals. There now, that ought to be it for phone calls for today, she mused after she hung up and put on the kettle for tea.

The next day she headed down to the police station to make sure nothing needed to be signed, then the pharmacy to see what was going on and to see if she was out of any product. The store was busy and everyone made quite a commotion when she walked in.

"Aye. Aye. Had a grand time, thank ye. Yes, we've picked a date. Aye, pretty exciting." She was trying to answer all the questions at once that were being thrown at her. After a few more minutes of interrogation, she was able to escape to the back to check out her department. When things quieted down, Jim made his way to the back.

"Really nice to have you back, Tess."

"Thank ye, Jim. It's sure nice to be home. As I said, I had a wonderful time. I seem to be like a fish out of water when I'm away from here."

Jim laughed. "So sounds like you won't be packing up and moving off to Winnipeg anytime soon."

"Ohhhh… let's not even go there! That is the one conversation the pair of us have been avoiding like the plague, I'm afraid." Tessy shook her head and kept on counting her stock. She was there for about an hour when Roger, who had been her postal carrier at one time, came in.

"Roger! How have ye been? Good to see ye. Oh, dear, I really miss seeing ye every day. How's Connie?"

"Hi, Tess, really good to see you, too. Connie is doing great, thanks. Yeah, it's just not the same since they've stopped residential mail service. I miss seeing everyone. I'm doing okay. They gave me a severance package, which was nice, but I've been going stir-crazy! That's why I applied for a job with the town."

"Oh, Roger. That's grand. Have ye heard anything?"

"Yep. Just heard today. Got the job."

"Congratulations, Roger. Couldn't be happier for ye."

"Well, you know that Ike is retiring next month after being with the town for forty years. So they were looking for someone who knew the town well and thought that I would be a good fit."

"Well, that's just grand, Roger. I bet Connie is tickled."

"Yeah, that's for sure. She was not looking forward to having me under foot all day," Roger chuckled.

Tessy laughed, gave him a hug, and they said their good-byes.

Roger turned on his way out and called back to her, "So we'll see you at Ike's retirement party three weeks from Saturday. It's at the hall."

"Aye. That ye will. Wouldn't miss it."

Tessy finished up at the store and decided to stop off at Sheree's Sidewalk Cafe to pick up some gift certificates for Tommy. As she was waiting for them to be written up, a lovely, young kindred spirit entered the cafe. She was obviously of Irish descent. Her alabaster complexion sported subtle freckles; her large eyes were the colour of sage; her nose was delicately tipped, and her lips were roseate. A long, thick, curly mane of auburn hair framed her face and flowed wildly over her shoulders. It was like Tessy had stepped back in time and was looking at her own reflection in the mirror. She stood stunned and silent as the girl cheerfully smiled at her and said, "Good afternoon."

Tessy finally gathered herself and returned an equally cheerful, "Good afternoon."

"Excuse me, but I was wondering if you knew where this address is," she asked while holding up a piece of paper to Tessy.

"Aye. You're very close. It's just across the way, there." Tessy motioned for her to come and look out the window. She pointed to a small empty shop across the street.

"Thank you, kindly. My name is Sage." The young girl smiled and held out her hand.

Tessy took it and immediately there was a shock between them. They laughed, then drew back their hands and shook them.

"Oooooo, must be dry here," Sage concluded.

"Aye," Was all that Tessy offered, knowing full well it was more than dry air that produces a spark such as that.

"Do you happen to know who owns that empty building?"

"Aye. It belongs to the town and they've been looking to either rent it out or sell it for quite some time, I believe."

"Wonderful!" The girl happily clenched her fists. "I found it on-line but it wasn't really clear as to who owned it. I was hoping to take a look at it."

"Well, now. Do ye see that brick building down on the corner?"

"Yes."

"Well, that's the town office. And if ye go in and speak to a lovely lass by the name of Janet, she'll be able to steer ye in the right direction, I'm sure."

"Thank you so much… ummm… "

"Oh, sorry, dear. Tessy is my name. Tessy McGuigan."

"Well. Thank you, Tessy McGuigan." As she went to shake hands again they both laughed and decided a wave would suffice.

"You're very welcome, dear. And good luck."

Tessy watched her walk down the street. Something… there is something about her.

Tessy was in the cafe for a while longer as she picked out some bagels to have on hand for her lunches. She was just leaving when she looked down the street and noticed Sage coming back her way. She waited for her to catch up.

"So… how did it go, dear?"

"Great! I'm meeting an Ike there tomorrow morning at 9 a.m. Can't wait to have a look."

"Grand. Just grand."

"So now, all I have to do is find a hotel or bed and breakfast or something for a couple of days. Do you have any suggestions?" Sage eagerly asked.

"Oh, my… there's an agri-show on right at the moment. I'm not sure you are going to find anything close by for the next few days."

"Oh… Well… I guess all I can do is head back to Regina tonight and return in the morning. Thanks for your help. Hopefully, I will see you soon." And she turned to walk away.

"Sage, dear. Wait. Please. Regina is over an hour away. That's a lot of driving. I have a very large house with plenty of room. You'd be more than welcome to come and spend a couple of days with me."

"Oh, Tessy! Thank you, but you don't even know me and you would open your home?"

"Aye. I'll admit it is a mite odd, but your soul knows when it's right. And I feel it is right for us both. I can see that ye have a tender aura about ye. So if ye are comfortable doing so, you are very welcome."

"Well, again, thank you. That would be lovely. If you are sure?" Sage eagerly accepted.

"Aye. Let's live on the edge," Tessy smiled.

Sage laughed. "On the edge, then! But if I'm going to be a guest in your home, you should, at least, know my full name." She stretched out her hand, "Sage Haggerty."

Tessy went pale.

"Tessy. What's the matter?"

Tessy just stared at her for a moment. "Haggerty is my mother's maiden name."

17
Soul Relations

Sage's car was parked just down the street, so they jumped in and made their way to Tessy's. She was quite relieved she had done her spring cleansing and was ready for company. When they pulled up the lane, Sage let out a soft gasp of delight. "Oh Tessy! How lovely."

"Thank ye. Welcome to Ashling Manor."

Once inside, Duke and Darby, who were most excited to learn of their new guest, greeted them. Sage made an extreme fuss over them and they became immediate best friends. Tessy finally calmed them down enough to put them outside. She helped with Sage's bags and showed her to the upstairs guest room at the far end of the hall from hers.

"I'm sure you will find this room very comfortable and the washroom is just down the hall on the left. There should be plenty of towels and whatnot. Help yourself to some of the natural herbal and oil products I've left in there. I make them all from scratch."

"Tessy, it's just perfect. Thank you, so much. And yes, I will definitely give them a try."

"Well, grand. No need to thank me, dear. I'll just leave you to get unpacked and freshened up while I go down to the kitchen and put on the kettle. When you're ready, just pop on down."

Sage couldn't believe her good fortune. She spun around in the Victorian embellished room like a little girl, then rushed over to the window, pulling open the lace curtains to look out. It faced onto what looked like it would be magnificent summer gardens. Someday, I will own a beautiful home, such as this. Ashling Manor, how gracious you are and how welcome and safe I feel. Thank you.

She did exactly what she was told to do. She unpacked and went to freshen up in the main bathroom. "Oooh, a claw tub!" she whispered as she ran her fingers around the edge of it. Then she proceeded to close her eyes and inhale some of Tessy's lotions and bath salts. "Heavenly!"

She didn't want to seem rude so she figured she better head down to the kitchen as quickly as possible. Wherever the kitchen is, was her thought as she skipped down the stairs. She reached the bottom landing and stopped to see if she could hear anything. Sounds like it's coming from back there, she concluded as she made her way down the hall and, Yes!, into the kitchen.

"Aye. There ye are, Sage. All settled in?"

"Yes, thank you. It's wonderful. May I help with anything?"

"No, thank ye, dear. I wasn't expecting company so I've just taken a frozen shepherd's pie out of the freezer. I always make a couple extra when I do them so as to have them on hand for just such an occasion."

"Oh, I love shepherd's pie. Both my grandma and my mom make awesome shepherd's pie."

"Well, I hope mine won't be a disappointment to ye," Tessy chuckled.

"Oh, I'm sorry. I hope I didn't offend you. I'm sure yours will be delicious."

Tessy just laughed. She was enjoying this young, free spirited girl. "Would ye like a tea, dear?"

"Yes. Please."

The two women sat comfortably at the table and chatted as if acquainted for many years.

"So, where is it you're from, Sage?"

"Cornwall, Ontario."

"Oh, Ontario is such a beautiful province. So lush."

"And so busy! That's why I decided to move out to the prairies. I love small towns, and Ladyslipper seems so relaxed and quaint. But I do miss my mom."

"Aye. That it is… most of the time. So your mam's still back there, then?"

"Yeah. We speak almost every day, though."

"And your dad?"

"Oh, he and Mom divorced years ago. He wasn't a very nice man. All of us kids were born in Ottawa, then when Mom and Dad split up, Mom changed our names to her maiden name, packed us up, and moved to Cornwall."

"Oh, I'm sorry to hear that. Your mam sounds like a strong woman."

"Yes. She sure is."

"So ye have siblings, then?"

"Yep, my older brother, Rowan, and younger sister, Saffron. They are still in the area so Mom keeps busy with them."

"Nice to see that ye are a close family."

"Yeah, we are. But I always seemed to be the adventurous one. Which drove Mom crazy!"

Tessy chuckled. "Aye. I'm sure it did."

"I can't help but notice that your mam has named ye all after fine herbs. Do ye have any idea why she would have done that?"

"Probably because she loves her herbs and so does my grandma. My mom's name is Rosemary and my grandma's is Rose. It's kind of a tradition, I guess?"

"Aye. And what a fine tradition it is." Tessy felt a stirring like maybe there might be more to it but left it at that.

"Tessy, you have such a warm home. It makes me feel so welcome. I love all the herbs you have hanging and the antiques. You must love herbs, too."

Tessy smiled. "Aye, that I do and, well, most of the antiques you see still get used in some way, shape or form. I believe some of the old ways are still the best ways."

"I'm sorry. Did I just offend you, again?" Sage flinched.

Tessy laughed. "No, dear. 'Twould take much more than that for you to ever offend me." She reached over and gave the sweet girl a hug, again feeling the tingle between them.

Sage sheepishly looked at her, "Thanks. Do you use all these herbs?" she innocently asked.

"Aye, dear. I do. I guess I've always been known as Ladyslipper's Wise Woman, but recently I was asked to develop a natural healing department at the local pharmacy. So now I prepare natural products of all sorts, plus order in all the herbs and oils for people to use on their own. I call it The Wee Nook of Herbals and Oils."

"Awesome!" Sage yelped.

Tessy looked stunned at her exuberance.

"Sorry. It's just that this is so amazing. I will be needing all sorts of oils and lotions and stuff for my business. And after I inhaled the samples in your bathroom, wow, I was hoping you would give out the recipes and show me how to make them, or I would pay you to make them up for me."

"I've been wondering what it is that ye were wanting to set up in that wee shop, but I wasn't sure ye were ready to share that yet. So, if ye don't mind me asking, what is it that ye have planned, dear?"

"I'm opening up a Natural Healing Centre. I will be offering massage therapy, reflexology, and Reiki, and I'm also a yoga instructor, which is a whole other story. Oh, and I'm signed up for a colour and sound therapy course next month in Regina, as well."

"Oh, my sweet girl! You are a spiritual soul sister. I knew there was a reason the universe has joined us together. As you can see, my passion is herbs, oils and crystals, but I am a Reiki master as well and perform reflexology and aromatherapy. So we do make a fine fit."

"Oh, Tessy! I feel like I'm home. This just couldn't be more perfect."

18
A History Lesson of Lore

There was no end to the conversations between the two soul sisters… the Crone and the Maiden. No subject was off limits. There were no shields nor guards, no judgment, just honesty and respect was present.

"Do ye have any idea where your mam's ancestors are from, Sage?"

"Ireland, I guess."

Tessy chuckled. "Aye. I would think. It's just that with our linked names I was wondering if we might have come from the same clan."

"Cool. Mom might know a little more. I can ask her if you like? Where do you come from?"

"I come from County Cork, Ireland. My forefathers settled there after a small clan branched off from the Ulster Haggertys in the north of Ireland back about the mid-18th century."

"Wow. That is so cool. How do you know all that?"

Tessy laughed at Sage's childlike wonderment. "Well, I guess from interest, research, and plenty of lore told to me as a child from my granny in Ireland. She loved to tell me great tales, especially while we were out harvestin' the garden."

"Do you think you'll be able to figure out where we came from?"

"Well, if your mam can help out in any way, we might be able to find out just where ye roots are buried."

They cleaned up the kitchen and steeped a pot of chamomile tea to take into the living room.

"Would ye like a wee fire to warm your bones, dear?"

"Yes. That would be wonderful. I love a roaring fire."

Tessy got the fire blazing nicely and sat in the wingback chair placed on one side of the hearth while Sage took the one on the other side. They enjoyed watching the fire in silence, sipping their tea, mesmerized by the dancing flames and the sound of the birch logs cracking and popping.

Sage broke the silence. "Tessy, would you tell me one of your grandmother's stories?"

Tessy smiled at the warm memories of those tales. It had been a long while since she had thought of them. "Aye. I suppose I could. Let me see… so many to choose from. I think I'll tell ye one of my favourites and, if it turns out we are related, it will be a story of your ancestry, too."

"This is the story that has been repeated and handed down through time in the light of many a blazing hearth. It is the love story of my great-great-great grandparents, Liam and Maggie Haggarty." Tessy smiled as she watched Sage curl her feet up under her and get cozy, her eyes wide with anticipation.

"Now, Liam Haggerty was a Celtic sea captain, rugged yet strikingly handsome. Living the hard life of the sea, he was extremely fit with broad shoulders and a smile to match. The lasses would swoon when he came to port; therefore, he was never lonely for female companionship. His homeport was Kinsale Harbour, an important naval base at the time, which meant it was very rowdy and rough on occasion. It was mid-May, and he had docked his ship, The High Priestess, for a few days to make some repairs before heading back out to the high seas. Being offshore for so long, he and his crew were looking forward to a few pints at their favourite pub on the wharf. The Whaler's Watch catered more to the likes of the fishermen of the sea rather than the naval lads. It had been a couple of months since Liam had been in, but it didn't take long before the maidens were standing 'round listening to his tales of the sea, and each hopin' she'd be his pick for this anchorage. A beautiful lass… much as yourself… " Tessy glanced over at Sage, "came over to place down his ale. He took one look at this bewitching beauty and knew, without a doubt, he wanted her more than any other. He smiled his broadest smile and with confidence asked her name. The other girls scowled as they watched with great disappointment. She just kept her head down, looked away, and hurried back to the bar for her next tray of drinks. She avoided that particular table as best she could. Aye, I may be a bar maid but that doesn't mean I have to associate with the clientele. Especially the likes of him, bold as he is handsome. He obviously is not in need of one more female in his clutches, she thought to herself.

"Liam tried his best to catch her attention but she continued to dodge him. When her shift was over and the bar had closed up, she wiped down the tables, counted her pay, and headed out into the fresh night air. She stopped to take in a full breath. She was tired. It had been a busy one and her feet were swollen and sore. She was glad she lived in the small upstairs flat just at the end of the street. She had only taken a few steps when a large figure appeared out from the shadows. Her heart began to pound and she looked around to see if there was anyone to help. Her adrenalin was pumping and she reached for the knife she always carried in her sash. She pulled it and positioned herself into a firm stance." Tessy cleared her throat and gave her best impression of her ancestor.

" 'Whoa, whoa… pretty colleen with no name.' Liam stepped into the light, held up his hands and smiled.

"The lass dropped her hand to her side but the knife remained in full view. 'Do ye not know better than to be scaring a girl half to death in the middle of the night?' she scolded him.

"He laughed. 'I'm sorry. Truly, that was not my intent, quite the opposite, indeed. I waited to make sure ye did arrive home safe and sound.'

" 'And what makes ye think I'd be needin' your assistance? I've been makin' it home just fine for the past few months without it.'

" 'Aye, I can see that you're quite a spirited and capable woman. But since I'm already here, could I not, at least, do the honourable thing and walk ye to your door?'

" 'I'm not sure honourable is what ye have on your mind, sir.'

" 'Oooh, a woman of conclusions, are ye?'

" 'With the harem of women flockin' ye as they do, what else would I be expected to conclude?'

" 'I can't be held responsible for what other people tend to do.'

" 'I am not going to spend another minute out here in the dark talkin' to the likes of you. Do as ye wish but don't be expectin' a huge thank ye for scarin' ten years off me life.'

"Liam laughed and stood waiting for her.

"Liam did walk her to her door that night, and when he stood tall over her and looked down with his soft smile and twinklin' eyes, he told her his name was Liam. Then, once again, he asked her name. She looked up at him, returned a faint smirk, and replied 'Maggie.' She then turned, went in and closed the door."

Tessy got up to stoke the fire.

"What happened next? Did they get together? I guess they must have… they are your great, great, great grandparents. But what happened? Is there more?" Sage was almost beside herself.

Tessy chuckled. "Aye, dear. There is more. Liam went slow and patient with Maggie. He knew she was worth the wait. Every night he was in port, he waited for her to get off work and walked her home. On her time off, they would stroll the pier and he would buy her little tokens of his affection as they passed the street merchants in the market square. They did, in time, fall deeply, passionately in love, and spent many a night in each other's arms.

"However, Maggie held a secret. And the longer she went on not telling Liam, the more it tore her apart. She was fleeing, and Kinsale had seemed like the perfect spot at the time. It was as far away from Ulster as she could get. Her father was a wealthy merchant in Derry and he had promised his beautiful daughter to a powerful Earl who was known to be a ruthless tyrant and old enough to be her grandfather. Days before the nuptials were to take place, she escaped with the help of one of her chambermaids, whom she hoped, with all her might, had escaped unharmed as well. She knew the Earl would not give up looking for her. Out of principle, not love, therefore, she must remain hidden. She was afraid of what Liam might do if he knew. She needed to keep Liam from harm. The Earl would not think twice of having him put to death. So she carried on with her facade and the pain that went with it.

"Liam had been out to sea for some time, but when he returned they spent every waking and sleeping moment together. Maggie was a beauty, for sure, and had plenty of men pining for her affections, but any smart man knew to keep their distance, for she was Liam's lass and was to be adored from afar but never to be touched. On his last voyage he purposely stopped in Galway to visit one of the finest jewelers in all of Ireland to have a ring designed and crafted to surprise Maggie.

"When he presented it to her she burst into tears. Liam was baffled but held her while she wept. Maggie could bear her secret no longer and spilled her heart. She saw the fire build in Liam's soft eyes to hatred, not for her, but for the unjustness that had befallen his beloved. He put the ring on her finger and vowed he would never let anything happen to her. She was free! She felt such relief and so much love. She felt no one could harm her now. They could start a wonderful life together and finally forget the past even existed.

"Liam had left port again and would be gone for a month. Maggie continued laying whiskey and ale down for the weary, thirsty fishermen of Kinsale, and life looked like it would just merrily go on forever. Liam had been gone just over a fortnight when she looked up and noticed four men come in to the pub, suited in colours and a coat of arms she was hoping never, ever to see again: The Earl's guards. She immediately ducked into the kitchen. Panic raged through her very soul. She had to get out of there and fast. She watched where they were seated, then slowly crept out of the kitchen and made her way along the far side of the crowded pub in the darkest shadows she could find.

"Just as she reached the door, one of the locals was on the way in and greeted her with a big friendly fuss, alerting everyone's glance to the entryway, including the four guards. Maggie pushed past him and ran as fast as she could. She didn't even turn to see if she was being followed. She ran to her flat, slammed the door, locked it and hid in the dark, panting and puffing. She was safe. She had just caught her breath and started breathing once more, when all of a sudden the door was kicked in and there they were, all four of them, rough and mean and ready to do what they had to. What they were instructed to do.

"Maggie fought as best she could, but they struck her and tied her hands and dragged her out into the street – but not before they ripped Liam's ring off her finger and threw it in the ashes of her hearth. The townspeople, her friends, all watched in horror as they threw her on to the back of a horse and rode off. They had to get word to Liam, but how?"

Tessy stopped again. She was thirsty and needed a drink of water. She looked over at the wide-eyed Sage and smiled.

"I'm going for a water, dear, would ye like anything?"

"That sounds good. I'll go with you. Wow, they had some life! I can't wait to see what happens next."

"Aye. It gets better."

They each returned with a glass of water and settled back into the living room, with Sage deciding to lounge on the couch. Tessy stirred the ashes, then laid a cozy throw over Sage and continued.

"Liam had barely anchored when the word got to him. He ran to the flat to see if there might be any clue as to where they had taken her. He looked down into the cold ashes and saw the ring. His blood boiled, his fists clenched. He bent down and picked up the last thing that had touched his Maggie. He kissed it, put it in his vest pocket and tore out of the flat. He rounded up a few of his toughest, most loyal crew, and they saddled up and headed in the direction that Maggie had last been seen. The first thing he needed to do was find out more about this Earl that had kidnapped his Maggie, and he knew just where to go to get such information. Liam's ship was not just a fishing vessel; he imported and exported goods in the slow months so, therefore, knew a great many merchants along the coast. There was one fellow in particular whom Liam knew well, and he seemed to know a little about everyone who was anyone. Liam would track down this man and find out what he needed to know."

Tessy looked over at Sage who was struggling to keep her eyes open. Poor dear. It had been a very long day and tomorrow would prove to be even longer, for sure.

"Sage, dear. Why don't you go up to bed? You're tired."

"But I want to hear what happens to Maggie. Liam must save her," she protested.

Tessy chuckled. "This tale is over two hundred and fifty years old. I think it can wait one more night for you to find out the answer."

"Okay. I guess you're right. Tomorrow is going to be a big day… I hope! Oh, and don't worry about waking me in the morning, I'll be up and going, for sure." She got up, folded the throw, placed it on the back of the couch, picked up her glass of water, and said goodnight.

"Good night, Sage. Sleep tight."

19
Kindred Acquaintances

Both Tessy and Sage were up early. Tessy headed down to the kitchen to get the coffee brewing and prepare a light breakfast for Sage before she left.

Sage came bouncing into the kitchen well rested and full of vigor.

"Good morning, Tessy. How are you this morning?"

"Good morning, dear. Fine, thank ye. How did you sleep? Well, I hope."

"Oh, yes! I had a wonderful sleep, although I did dream of Maggie. It was just like being there… all the sights, the sounds, the smell of the salty air. It was quite exciting."

"Oh, my. That sounds more intriguing than relaxing." Tessy silently wondered whether Sage had actually dreamt it, or whether she had done some astral travelling through the night.

Sage giggled, then headed straight to the animals, spending a few minutes lavishing them with affection.

"Would ye prefer tea or coffee this morning, dear?"

"I think I will start with a coffee. Thank you."

"I've set out some bagels, cream cheese, fresh fruit and yogurt, with a variety of nuts to choose from. I thought maybe ye'd like to start out with some light fare before ye go, and then when ye get back I was thinking a nice spinach quiche for brunch to celebrate."

"That sounds perfect. Thank you. I really hope there is a reason to celebrate, though."

"It will all work out just fine. You'll see."

They finished breakfast and visited until it was time for Sage to go.

"Wish me luck," Sage nervously smiled as she stood at the door.

"Luck will not have a thing to do with it. If it is meant to be, the Universe has already set it in motion. Now, please say hi to Ike for me. Let him know that ye're staying here with me. I've known him and his lovely family for years. Taught two of his boys, I did."

"Certainly. Well, guess I'd better get going. I don't want to be late. And Tessy… thanks… for everything." Sage reached for a reassuring hug, turned, and skipped down the steps.

Tessy watched her drive out the lane. She had a really good feeling about Sage's shop and knew that she would do well in Ladyslipper. Then she started to laugh. "Oh, my!" She picked up Merlin, who had since forgiven her, trying to hide her giggle in his fur.

She just realized that the shop Sage was looking to rent was right next door to Chamberlain Agencies! Margaret Chamberlain's husband, Donald, owned and operated the insurance agency, and Mrs. Chamberlain was constantly popping in to see her husband about one thing or another. Having someone like Sage just a few steps away every day would surely throw her into a complete tizzy! Tessy felt guilty laughing. But, she reflected, *I feel it will prove to be quite a predicament for, at least, a while. I really should give Sage a heads-up just in case she runs into Mrs. Chamberlain, although I do not want to start a squabble before one appears. Aye, I must deal with this as discreetly as possible.*

While Sage was gone, Tessy decided she would pop over to the Bakers' and deliver the gift certificates to Tommy. When she arrived Betty greeted her at the door and told her that Danny and Tommy were out picking up some supplies and wouldn't be back for a time. Tessy wanted to present them in person to properly thank Tommy for watching over things for her and to apologize for the mishap with Mrs. Chamberlain, so she asked Betty if she would ask Tommy to drop over later. She didn't mention that she also thought it might be nice for Tommy and Sage to meet. Both being fairly new to town, they might just hit it off grand.

About an hour later, Sage came bounding through the door.

"Tessy, I'm going to take it! It's just perfect!"

"Oh, that's grand, Sage, dear. Congratulations. I couldn't be happier."

"Boy, Ike is sure a nice man. He certainly thinks the world of you, too. He said he's actually not going to be working for the town much longer. That's too bad."

"Aye. A fine man, he is. Glad to see him retire while he's still able to get about and do some travellin'. He and his wife, Gloria, have worked hard all their lives. Raised a fine family, bless their souls."

"I'm going to love it here. Everyone is so friendly."

You just hold that thought, dear, was the first thing to come to Tessy's mind, but she remained silent.

Sage went up to her room to get changed into something more comfortable and to phone her mom to give her the good news. When she came back down, Tessy was taking the quiche out of the oven.

"Ahhh… just in time, dear."

"Boy, that looks as great as it smells!"

"Thank ye. Now, let's hope it tastes every bit as good. Sit. Sit. Have it while it's hot."

They sat and enjoyed their chat as much as their quiche.

"So, I imagine your mam was happy for ye."

"Yes and no. I think she was really hoping I wouldn't like it here and come home."

"Aw. Bittersweet, was it, then?"

"Yeah. She tried to sound happy for me but I could tell."

"Well, maybe she could come have a visit with ye, and then she would probably feel better about ye being here."

"That would sure be nice. I did tell her all about you, though, and she said to say thank you very much for looking out for me.

She said she would like to talk to you sometime so she could thank you herself."

"Aye. That would be lovely. No need to thank me, but I would love to have a chat with her and maybe help put her mind at ease."

"I forgot to ask her about our heritage, though. Darn. I was so excited about my shop. I'll ask her tomorrow when I call her."

"That's fine, dear. Your heritage is not going anywhere between now and then."

"I love the way you put things," Sage chuckled.

Tessy had invited Sarah and Cherokee over for an afternoon class before she had known anything about entertaining a houseguest. She was going to reschedule, but decided this would be a wonderful opportunity for the girls to get to know Sage. It would also introduce them to a young entrepreneur starting up a business in natural healing, thus confirming there is a future in the field upon which they were planning to embark.

After introductions were made, Sarah and Cherokee fired non-stop questions at Sage: "Where did you take your classes?" "How long did it take?" "What's your favourite field?" "Why?" "What's next?" Sage didn't mind in the least, and seemed to quite enjoy sharing and reliving her journey to success. She even popped out to her car to retrieve a box full of her textbooks and notes, offering to lend them if they wished. Tessy smiled as she witnessed the bond developing between the three like-minded young lasses. *The Universe does steer us to the same path when the time is right.* Filled with gratitude she added, *thank you for this blessing.*

The afternoon merrily flew by. When the girls weren't talking about alternative healing, they were excitedly discussing plans for Sarah's upcoming sixteenth birthday celebration. Sage, who had already been invited, contributed some wonderful suggestions, and although she was eight years their senior, she was eager to participate. She, in turn, invited Sarah and Cherokee to drop by her shop any time they wished, and the girls offered to help her move in and set up. Aye… it was a good match made, the three of them.

When it was time for the girls to leave, Sage and Tessy walked them to the door and were saying their good-byes when there was a knock. The girls, being closest to it, opened it to find Tommy standing there. The sight of a foyer filled with females almost sent the bashful Tommy fleeing. He stumbled back, turned beet red, bowed his head and stammered, "Oh, I'm sorry to interrupt. Betty said for me to come over. But I see you're busy. I'll just come back another time." And he started to turn and escape.

"Tommy! Tommy, dear, wait." Tessy was starting out the door to fetch him back.

Cherokee piped up. "It's okay, Tommy. We were just leaving. Come on back. Bye, Sage, Tessy. Probably see you tomorrow." And the girls headed down the walk past Tommy.

Tommy turned back to notice Sage still standing at the door. He wasn't sure what to do. He stood, frozen by her beauty. Tessy broke the silence. "Tommy, please come in. I'd like you to meet Sage."

Sage radiated a bright smile and stretched out her hand. "Hi. I take it you're Tommy, nice to meet you. I'm Sage."

Tommy gently took her hand and nodded his head. "Yes… hummm… nice to meet you, too, Sage."

Tessy turned to hide a stir of elation.

As Tommy refused to come in, saying he was just out on some errands, Tessy quickly thanked him for looking after things while she was away and profusely apologized for the unfortunate run-in with Mrs. Chamberlain. She then left Tommy and Sage alone for a few minutes while she went to retrieve the gift certificates.

It was a brief first encounter but, Tessy felt, an important one just the same.

After he left, Sage peeked out the lace curtains and said, "He's pretty cute."

Tessy smiled and put her arm around Sage's shoulder. "Aye, that he is."

20

The Tale's End

After all the company had left, Tessy and Sage prepared a bite to eat. They had almost finished their supper when Sage asked, "May we go into the living room and continue on with the story of Liam and Maggie when we are done here?"

Tessy smiled. "Aye, dear. We certainly may."

Sage could hardly wait. While she quickly cleared the table and put all the dishes in the dishwasher, Tessy put on the kettle for their tea. Soon they were snuggled in front of another cozy fire and Tessy continued on with her tale. "Let's see… where was I? Aye…

"Liam and his men saddled up and were now on their way to Cork. That is where Liam's well-informed friend was stationed, and that is where he would, hopefully, find out the information he was seeking regarding this tyrant who'd had Maggie tracked down and kidnapped. It was already late in the day and they had a three-hour ride to Cork, so when they arrived at the inn on the outskirts of the city, Liam told his men they would spend the night there and get a good start in the morning. He appreciated that his men would have kept on riding if that is what he wanted, but they had just docked from a long month off shore, and now this. He knew they were tired. He arranged rooms for his men and instructed them to eat, drink and rest well tonight, for he wasn't sure when they would be this comfortable again. He sent a messenger to seek out his merchant friend, Eoin, and request a meeting with him early in the morning.

"Liam and his men did eat, drink and rest well that night. The next morning, while they were just finishing their breakfast, Liam's friend arrived. Liam instructed his men to get the horses saddled up and ready to go, and to load enough food and supplies to last at least a couple of days. Now that Liam and Eoin were alone they could speak freely. Liam found out everything he needed to know about this scoundrel, and more. Enough information to make sure this low-life rat would never bother his Maggie or him ever again.

"Eoin also told him of a crone he should visit along his way. She lived about four hours along on their ride, and only about a quarter hour out of their way past the mighty rock. However, a very worthwhile stop, he assured Liam. 'If anyone knows where your Maggie is, it will be the crone,' he said. 'Tell her I've sent ye. Make sure ye leave her a few coppers, is all.' Liam thanked his friend and told him he would gladly repay him with free cargo on his next shipping anytime, anywhere, and for his friend to come and rejoice in a wedding. For, he vowed, there would be a wedding when he returned with Maggie. They shook hands and bade farewell.

"With his men and horses well rested, they rode hard and fast. About three and a half hours later, Liam started looking for the signs of where he was told to turn off to see the crone. He would go alone, leaving his men to wait on the main road. They came to the huge rock at a fork in the road where a small path led off to the right. This must be it, Liam thought to himself. 'You men stay here and rest the horses,' he told his men. 'I'll be back shortly.' And he rode off down the little trail.

"He soon came upon a little cottage built into a hill with the sod continuing over it and a couple of goats lazily grazing on the roof's sweet grasses. An old woman came to the door. 'What is it that ye want?' She glared as she wiped her hands on the edges of her skirt. There was a large Irish wolfhound standing at her side, almost reaching her height, silent but very alert.

" 'I mean you no harm, ma'am. Eoin has sent me.'

" 'Eoin is it. Well, then. Come, come.' She turned and went into the little dwelling, and Liam dismounted, tied his horse and followed her in.

" 'Come. Sit,' said the crone. 'Why is it that Eoin is sending ye to my door?' She leaned over a large black pot suspended over the fire, stirring its contents.

" 'Some men have come and kidnapped my lady and I am on my way to find her and bring her home.'

" 'Hmmmm. And what is your lady's name, sir?'

" 'Maggie. Maggie O'Donnell.'

" 'Hmmmm. And do ye have anything that Maggie O'Donnell has touched or worn recently?'

"Liam thought for a moment. The ring! I have her ring. 'Aye. Yes. Here. I have the ring that she wore.' He reached into his vest pocket and handed it to the old woman.

"The crone took the ring, closed her eyes and held it tightly in her hand. 'Aye… I see her. She is well. Hmmm… she's fiery, that one. They've had a time with her.'

Liam laughed. 'Aye. They'll not want to get her temper up, that's for sure. Can you see where she is? Where they have taken her?'

" 'They've not yet reached their destination. They've stopped. Carry on to where ye are headed. They are on the coast. Ye will catch up with them there. But… ye must hold off trying to rescue her in the city. Ye must wait until ye're past, in the quiet glens of Connaught. Aye… that is where ye will reunite. Now, mind… ye might think ye should take the path well trod, but do not… take the path less travelled and ye shall win your prize. Now, go. Water your horse and be gone with ye.' She handed the ring back to Liam, turned and continued on with the contents of her pot.

"Liam got up. 'Thank ye kindly, ma'am. I am in your debt.' He lay a small pouch of coins on the table and left. The hound was the only one that watched him leave.

Sage interrupted. "Tessy, I have to go to the bathroom, and then I am going to go get my jammies on. If that's okay."

"Aye, dear. That's fine. I'll take our cups to the kitchen, then. Would you like anything?"

"Yes! Do you have any of those awesome brownies left?"

Tessy laughed. "Aye, I think there are a couple left that I could bring in for us."

"Oh, thank you. Yes, please."

Tessy was waiting in the big chair when Sage returned. She got cozy on the couch, pulled the throw up over her, and grabbed a brownie off the plate. "Okay… ready," she said, bright eyed.

Tessy laughed. "Well, now… When Liam returned to his men, he explained as best he could that they needed to carry on and that they would be successful in their venture. The men, not really knowing what had just taken place, looked at one another, shrugged, and continued on. Liam's top crewman and best friend, Rory, rode close to Liam, 'Liam, who was it that ye were talkin' to back there? Where is it ye got this message?'

"Liam was an honest man and would never consider lying to his friend, so he explained about the crone and what she told him.

" 'And ye believe what this old woman had to say?'

" 'Aye. 'Tis the best lead we have so far,' Liam laughed, slapped his friend on the shoulder, and rode on ahead.

"It was getting late, so Liam decided they would make camp for the night and carry on to Limerick the next day. They made a small fire and cooked some fish that two of the lads had caught while the others set camp. After they ate, one of the crew pulled out his penny whistle and played them some tunes before they bedded down. In the morning they were up early and reached Limerick in good time. They headed straight to the town square to replenish their supplies. While there, Liam asked the street merchants a few questions. He found out there had been a couple of guards with a woman of Maggie's description in town about eight days earlier, supposedly heading to Galway. Liam ordered his men to mount up and they were off. So they are on the coast. The crone was right, Liam thought as they rode out of town. He would definitely pay attention to her instructions from this point on.

"They spent another night under the stars before reaching Galway. Liam planned on spending a couple of days here finding out what he could. Again, being a coastal city, he had many a friend he could rely on. They headed to their favorite inn on the bay and got settled before Liam proceeded down to the docks to see what he could find out. As it turned out, some guards and a woman were staying at an inn in the heart of the square.

"Liam couldn't believe his luck. He must go immediately. He didn't want to attract any attention, so decided not to include his band yet, but he did stop off to pick up Rory and they headed to the center of town. They checked a few of the inns down in the main area and didn't have any luck. They were standing on the corner deciding which one to check next when they heard a big ruckus across the street in one of the upstairs rooms, and a couple of objects came flying out the window. Liam could see his Maggie! She was all fired up and throwing things at someone. He wanted to laugh and cry at the same time. He grabbed Rory's arm and pulled him into the alley. He didn't want Maggie to see them and accidentally alert the guard.

" 'We have to go about this very carefully. Now that we have found her we must not let her out of our sight but not let her see us, either.'

" 'Liam. What has gotten' in to ye? Let's just go and get her. There is only two of them. We can take them. No problem. Especially if we take them by surprise.'

" 'No. We can't. The crone said to wait until they were out of the city. Then we will get her.'

" 'What are ye talkin' about, man? Are ye daft? She's right there.'

" 'Aye. Don't ye think I want to go get her? But the crone has been right so far, and I'm not going to mess it up now. We wait. I'll stay; you go tell the others what has happened and set up watch times for everyone.'

"Rory knew when Liam had his mind set there was no backing down.

"So it was that for the next three days Maggie and her captors were secretly watched night and day. It turned out that two of the guards had gone on ahead to Galway on business for the Earl; then they had met up with the other two who were left to watch Maggie. They finally finished up with their dealings, and it looked like they were getting prepared to leave. Word was sent back to Liam, and they, too, were packed up and ready to go upon a moment's notice. Sure enough, the next morning the guards tied Maggie on her horse and they were off. Liam and his men lagged behind but kept them in view. Liam told his men to keep their distance while he and Rory went on ahead to make sure Maggie stayed in sight. They came to the fork in the road where the guards had taken the main route. Liam instinctively knew this was where he should take the path less travelled. He turned his horse in the other direction.

" 'Where in the devil are ye going, man?' Rory barked.

" 'We're going this way. Come on.'

"Rory shook his head and followed his friend. The rest of the band finally caught up and, not knowing Liam and Rory had taken the other path, headed down the main roadway. This is exactly what Liam had planned. With his band of men behind the guards and he and Rory taking the short cut past them, they would create the perfect ambush.

"About an hour in, Liam and Rory were able to see the guards and Maggie. They had stopped on the edge of the road, undoubtedly for one of the guards to relieve himself. They were very close. Liam held up his hand for Rory to stop. They both got off their horses.

Liam caught a glimpse of something moving off in the far direction. It was the rest of his crew. It was now or never. He waited a few moments for his men to creep closer, then he signaled. That startled a family of pheasants that fluttered up to the highest branches. All of a sudden there was yelling, arrows flying, then the sound of swords and knives slashing. When it was all over, there were three guards slain, and one wounded but still alive.

"Liam stood over him. 'I will spare your life. Deliver this letter to the Earl. Tell him Maggie and I best not see or hear of him ever again, or I will see to it that the information I have will go straight to the King, and he will surely be tried for treason. Now, get on your horse and be gone before I change my mind and deliver the message myself.'

"Liam ran over to Maggie, untied her and pulled her down from the horse. They hugged and kissed and she cried in his arms. They returned to Kinsale and were married within the next fortnight. Their youngest son, of their five children, was my great, great, great grandfather, Eoin Desmond Haggerty."

Sage wiped away some tears and remained silent for a moment, hugging a large pillow she had adopted during Liam's rescue of Maggie. Then she brightened and piped, "Hey! He was named after the merchant that gave Liam the information!"

"Aye."

"Wow. That is amazing. Did that really happen? Is that really true about your ancestors? Maybe my ancestors?"

"Aye, dear. As true a fact as my granny told to me and as it was told to her."

Sage, still in a state of awe, soon said her goodnights and went upstairs to bed.

As Tessy turned out all the lights, she wondered whether Sage would have a peaceful sleep or possibly travel to another time filled with romantic adventure.

21

Maybe Dabblin' a Mite

The next morning, after breakfast, Sage went for a walk. Tessy decided she would give Marshall a call. They hadn't spoken in a couple of days, and he knew nothing about Sage, so she thought she should get him up to speed on what was going on. She poured herself a coffee and dialed his number.

"Good morning. Tayse residence."

"Mornin' Dotty, dear. It's Tessy."

"Morning, Tessy. How are you?"

"Just grand, thanks. How are you and Bert?"

"Everything's great, here. Sure miss you."

"Thanks. I miss you, too. Is the good doctor about?"

"Yes. I believe he is in the study. I'll just let him know you're on the phone. Take care."

"Well, hello, my lady. What an unexpected surprise. I've been thinking about you. I was planning on giving you a call in a bit."

"Nice to see I'm still in your thoughts but a mite quicker on the draw, love," Tessy chuckled.

Marshall laughed. "Oh, you think so, do you?"

"Aye."

"What's up? Something is on your mind. I can always tell."

"Ye think you're so smart. Well, to be perfectly honest, there has been a bit of excitement around here. I've had a house guest for the past couple of days."

"A house guest! What kind of a house guest?"

Tessy chuckled. "A lovely young lass by the name of Sage Haggerty. She is going to be opening a little shop here in Ladyslipper."

"Haggerty? Wasn't that your mother's name?"

"Aye, 'twas. Quite odd, isn't it?"

"Very! Seems I can't leave you alone for a minute without you getting into some kind of mischief. How did she end up staying with you?"

"Well, she needed a place to stay and I had plenty of room. And I certainly wouldn't call it mischief."

Marshall laughed. "No, I guess not. Will she be staying with you long?"

"Not quite sure, at this point. I am assuming we will be discussing that very soon."

"Well, you seem to be enjoying her, so that's good."

"Aye. She's just a lovely, sweet girl. Sarah and Cherokee met her yesterday and the three of them got along famously."

"How old is she?"

"I'd say probably around 24 years. Oh, and, I also introduced her to young Tommy."

There was a moment of silence. "You wouldn't be dabbling in a little matchmaking, would you, dear?"

"Matchmaking? Really! I just thought that two nice young people, who just happened to both be from down east and new to Ladyslipper, might have something in common. I just introduced them. What happens after that is none of my affair."

Marshall chuckled. "Yes, I suppose. Look what happened to us."

"Aye. That wasn't all so bad, now, was it?"

"Well, I never quite know what to expect when you call, but I must admit it wasn't this. Like I said, it sounds like you are really enjoying your company, so good for you. I look forward to meeting her on my next trip out."

Tessy and Marshall chatted for a while longer, discussing wedding plans and everyday matters. When they hung up, Tessy decided to go to the library and have a little chat with Dermot. She was wondering if Dermot was, in any way, responsible for Sage being in the picture.

"Let's just see what ye have to say 'bout all this, Dermot, my love," she said out loud as she opened the library doors.

She stood quiet for a few moments waiting for Dermot to guide her. She slowly scanned the room for any clues. Nothing seemed out of place until she noticed a small white feather lying on the cover of one of her Aunt's photo albums. She went over, picked up the feather, then the album, and sat in the big armchair. She turned the pages, softly stroking them, experiencing the energy – the memories – they produced. She closed her eyes. Something… there was something she was missing. Just then she heard the front door open as Sage came bounding into the house.

"Tessy. Tessy, I'm back."

"In here, dear," Tessy called out as she closed the album and placed it back on the little table.

Tessy met Sage in the hall. "Well, how was your wee jaunt?"

"It was great. I am going to love Ladyslipper! I walked down town and just stood in front of my shop and imagined all the wonderful things that are going to happen here."

Tessy laughed. "Aye, dear. I, too, feel that you are going to do just grand. Come to the kitchen and I'll make us some tea while you tell me all about it."

"I stopped in at the town office and made an appointment to sit down with Ike and get all the paperwork done. He mentioned that since they have been trying to rent or sell it for so long there is a possibility that I could rent to own. Can you imagine, Tessy! And, if that happens, there is a space upstairs that I think I could turn into a darling little apartment. It needs quite a bit of work, but I'm sure I could find someone to do some handy work for me. Do you know of anyone, Tess?"

Tessy knowingly grinned as she poured the water into the teapot. "Aye. I can think of one who is very handy and probably able to give you a fair amount of his time for a fair price."

"That's awesome. You'll have to introduce me to him as soon as everything is finalized and we can get started. The sooner we get going, the sooner I can be out of your hair."

"You're not at all in my hair, dear. You're welcome to stay as long as ye need. And ye have already met this handyman."

"No! You don't mean Tommy?"

"Aye. I certainly do. He's the most reliable, hardworking young man I know. What's wrong with having Tommy help ye?"

"No. He's way too cute and I can't imagine having him so close every day! He'd be working for me. That would be awful."

Tessy chuckled. "He'd be helping ye out, and that's just the way ye'd have to look at it. With a bit of money exchanged, is all."

"Can't you think of anyone else?" Sage begged.

"Not that would be able to work for ye, at the drop of a hat, like this. And certainly not for the same wages as, I'm sure, Tommy will charge ye. Danny won't be needin' him full time until spring so he's definitely your best bet."

"Ohhhhh… I'll have to think about it. But thanks," pouted Sage.

Tessy smiled and handed her a tea.

22
Stumbling into the Future

For the next week, life at Ashling Manor carried on with a flow of normality. Tessy spent a couple of days at the pharmacy catching up. On one of the mornings, Sage went with her to check out which of Tessy's products she would like to incorporate into her shop. That same afternoon, she was meeting Ike to finalize all the paperwork and pick up the keys.

"Oh Tessy! I can't believe this is really happening. My very own shop!"

"Aye, dear. It is an exciting time, for sure. Come. I'll treat ye to lunch before ye head off."

"Thanks Tessy. That sounds wonderful, but I'm not sure I'll be able to eat anything. Although, you know me… I'll give it a good try," Sage giggled.

After lunch, Tessy returned to the pharmacy and Sage went off to sign the rent to own papers and take possession of her new property. When she left the town office, she was so elated she literally ran down the street and burst into the pharmacy looking for Tessy, and ran smack dab into Tommy, almost knocking him over. She hit him with such force that she bounced back and he had to quickly grab her arm so she did not hit the floor.

"Oh! I am so sorry!" she exhaled as she covered her embarrassed face with her hands.

"That's okay," Tommy chuckled, actually relieved to see he wasn't the only one that got embarrassed over stuff like this.

"No. I should have been more careful and watching where I was going. I'm so sorry," she repeated.

"Sage… Really, it's okay."

"Thanks. I was just coming to get Tessy to show her my new shop… across the street… over there… but I don't see her so maybe I'll just go…" Sage scrunched her face, realizing she was babbling on as she flimsily waved her pointed finger over her shoulder towards her shop and nodded her head up and down.

Tommy was smiling at her and nodding his head in unison. "Congratulations. That's great."

"Thanks. Okay, then. I'm just gonna go, now… " Sage nodded while backing up towards the door, narrowly missing an incoming customer.

"Okay, then. See ya," Tommy repeated, still smiling and nodding as well.

"Yeah. See ya." Sage brightly smiled, turned and slunk out the door. *That's it. I for sure cannot have him work on my shop now*, she thought as she hurried across the street. She heard her name being called from down the way and turned to see Tessy rushing toward her.

"Sage. Sage, dear," she called, waving her arms.

"Hi, Tessy," Sage returned, as she inserted the key into the front door of her new life.

"What's the matter, dear. I thought you'd be beside yourself."

"Well, I was until I mowed over Tommy in the pharmacy just now."

"Oh my… " Tessy giggled.

"Yeah. He thought it was pretty funny, too. I'm so embarrassed! What a way to screw up the best day of my life."

"Now, now, dear. It's not all that bad. Don't let a little mishap dampen your spirits. You of all people should know you must always keep your spirits high."

"You're right. Moving on… Now… look at this! Isn't it amazing? Over here will be the reception and waiting area. This first room will be for massage and reflexology, and the one at the end will be my Reiki and sound and colour therapy room."

Sage's excitement heightened with every turn into a different room. They went to the back area and up the stairs to what would eventually become her new home. All week she had been envisioning how it would look with this here and that there. Now all she had to do was find someone to make those visions turn into a reality.

"I guess I had better start looking for someone to help me get going on the renovations," Sage thought out loud.

"Well, did ye mention it to Tommy when you ran into him?" Tessy winced, then gave the recovering Sage an apologetic glance. "Sorry, dear. No pun intended."

"It's okay. And no. I certainly did not say a word to him nor am I going to."

"Sage, dear. Don't let your ego get in the way of starting your new life as it is meant to be. Besides, you'd be doing him as much a favour as he'd be doing you. Tommy could definitely do with a little extra cash. He's been saving up for a vehicle so he can return to mechanics school. Look! There he is now just up the street. Away ye go and have a wee chat with him."

Sage looked at Tessy and hesitated for a moment, then ran down the stairs and out the front door. A few minutes later, Sage and Tommy were in the shop wandering from room to room discussing renovations. Tessy met them in the reception area, excused herself, and left them alone to launch whatever outcome the future was deemed to embrace.

It was almost suppertime when Sage entered Ashling Manor. Tessy was in the kitchen, and turned to see a calm and blissful young lass. Sage walked over to Tessy, put her arms around her and said, "Thank you. I am so glad you told me to suck it up and not let my ego get in the way. Tommy is awesome! We have so much in common. And I'm not just talking about renovations."

Tessy smiled, returned the hug and said, "That's grand, dear. Just grand."

23
A Full March

March was proving to be a busy month!

Sage and Tommy spent a great deal of time together, both in and out of the shop. Sarah's sixteenth birthday celebration was a huge success with the party for the young people being Sage and Tommy's first official date. There was Ike's retirement party to attend. And Tessy had two significant merrymakings, St. Patrick's Day and Ostara, to prepare for. Yes, it was a very full month.

Marshall had planned on making it for the family portion of Sarah's birthday gala; however, a patient emergency made it impossible for him to arrive on time. He did arrive a week later, lavishing Sarah with a multitude of gifts. He could stay only a few days, but it was long enough to escort Tessy to Ike's retirement party, and he was especially glad that it would be time enough to help Tessy celebrate St. Paddy's Day. Most people assumed that Tessy enjoyed this particular day simply because she was Irish. And she did. However, she also discreetly delighted in the hidden meaning of the three-leaved clover: love, fertility and wisdom… Maiden, Mother, Crone.

While Marshall was in Ladyslipper he had a chance to meet Sage and Tommy. He was quite taken with them both.

"I can certainly see why you have befriended them and had your hand in their courtship. They seem very well matched," he confided to Tessy one evening when they were alone and snuggled by the fire.

Marshall had not been staying with Tessy as Sage was still residing at Ashling Manor while Tommy was working on her apartment, and they thought it might prove a little awkward. Also, Marshall had not yet discussed with Penny what effects she thought it might have on the kids.

While enjoying their alone time they confirmed a few unfinished wedding details and went over the guest list one more time, adding two new friends to it. There was a lull in the conversation, and that was when Tessy decided to bite the bullet and bring up the one thing they had been avoiding.

"Marshall, love. We must talk about our permanent living arrangements before we go any further. I know it's something that has been plaguing us both."

"You are so right, darling. And I'm sorry. It's not good to keep this dangling on. And I actually have some news I've been waiting to share with you. My new colleague and I have been talking things over this past week, and he was wondering if I could stay on until next January. He would be able to take over completely at that time and then I could fully retire. I told him I would discuss it with you and let him know. But, unfortunately, that would mean I wouldn't be able to make any permanent changes until then. What do you think?"

"Oh, my! Next January! That's quite a ways away." Tessy was in a slight state of shock.

"Darling. It doesn't mean we can't go ahead with all our plans. It's just that our actual living arrangements will have to remain pretty much the same as they are now."

"Oh. Yes. I suppose."

"Tessy, I don't want this to upset you. Please. We must just keep forging ahead with our preparations. I don't want this to ruin anything."

Tessy gathered her thoughts to a more positive outlook, smiled up at Marshall, then calmly answered, "No, love. It won't ruin a thing. It will just allow us a bit more time to adjust and prepare to share the rest of our lives together. However… you must promise me one thing. That you will stop getting so long-in-the-jaw every time we separate. It's just going to be a fact of life for the next while. So… are we agreed, then?"

"Agreed," Marshall sheepishly answered. They shook on it, then he leaned down and kissed his love.

The next morning Tessy was in the kitchen getting her recipe out for her Irish stew when the phone rang.

"Good mornin' to ye," she gleefully answered.

"Tessy. Is that you?" was the reply.

"Aye. Eileen Tucker, is it?"

"Yes. Yes. How are you? Just wanted to call to say Happy St. Patrick's."

"Well, dear. Thank ye kindly. Happy St. Paddy's to you, as well. How have ye been?"

"Great! Couldn't be better. Having the time of my life!"

"Well, grand. Glad to hear it."

"Yep… going to an Irish wingding tonight. In fact, been out every night this week. Then Monday there's a group of us heading for Vegas. Can't wait."

"My, look at you. Things must be going well. Glad to see you're getting out and about, but are ye sure you're not overdoing it?"

"Hell, no! I'm just getting started."

"Eileen, dear. How much of that tea are ye drinkin' a day?"

"Probably two or three cups. That's another reason I'm calling. I'm getting low and I'll need some more. So if you could just whip me up a batch I'll be glad to pay you and, of course, for the shipping."

"Aye. I could make some up but I think I'll have to tone it down a mite if you're going to be drinking that much a day."

"Well don't be tampering with it too much. It's a miracle, that stuff. Haven't felt this good in years, maybe ever! Even got myself a couple of gentlemen callers! That perfume you gave me works like a charm! They might not be able to hear worth a damn, but there certainly isn't anything wrong with their sense of smell."

Tessy chuckled. "That's grand, Eileen. Just grand."

They chattered for a few minutes more, made arrangements for her new batch of tea, then ended the conversation with Eileen heading off to get her hair done.

A wide-eyed Tessy chuckled again, shook her head and said to Merlin, "My, I hope we haven't created a monster. I will be toning down that tea, for sure, before she lands in the grave!"

Tessy's St. Patrick's Come and Go celebration consists of a huge crockery filled with Irish stew, herbed soda bread biscuits, non-stop Celtic music, festive pots of shamrocks, and a variety of beers – none of which are green! The only green refreshment she serves is her Leprechaun's Limelight drink for the children. The festivities commence around 11 a.m. and trail off about 8 p.m. This year she placed a statue of a gleeful leprechaun beside her fountain at the front door to greet her guests and set the mood. Beside him sat a cauldron filled with bags of chocolate coins wrapped in gold foil for the children to help themselves to on their way home.

The day was filled with well-wishes of old Irish blessings, songs, love and laughter. Marshall was enjoying it immensely. It reminded him of his first outlandish celebration at Ashling Manor, Christmas in July! That was his first glimpse of Tessy and the last he saw of his heart. He watched her today as he watched her then; she was gracious, fun and giving. Love fell out of her every pore with ease, and soon he was about to be married to this lovely creature of God. He was starting to get choked up with gratitude, so he shook the thoughts from his head and went to see if he could help with the children's activities.

People joyously came and went throughout the day, experiencing their wee taste of the Emerald Isle. The hour was getting on, the crock was draining, the beer was diminishing, and there had been enough good cheer to last a healthy while. Tessy and Marshall bade farewell to the last of the stragglers and watched them climb into a taxicab, before they closed the door for the evening. Sage and Tommy were in the kitchen washing dishes.

"Tessy, that was a blast!" Sage greeted them as they came in. "I'm going to miss Ashling Manor so much. There always seems to be something going on here."

"Well, dear. It's not goin' anywhere. When ye get moved in to your apartment, it doesn't mean you'll no longer be welcome at my door."

They finished tidying up, and Sage and Tommy decided to get some fresh air and take Duke and Darby for a walk. Tessy and Marshall were alone once more. They both were tired after the day's festivities and snuggled on the couch. They were relieved they had finally discussed and come to a resolution regarding their living arrangements. It had put to rest the unsettling tension that had been building between them, and they were now on their path back to unwavering love and compatibility. Even though Marshall was leaving the next day, they laughed and teased with ease. When it was time for Marshall to go, they stood in the foyer holding tight to one another. As always, it was difficult, but now at least less complicated. Their relationship was definitely back on solid ground. Tessy watched him drive away, closed the door, looked in the mirror, and with gratitude said, "You are a blessed woman."

Sage had been begging Tessy to teach her how to make some herbal products, so for the next few days they busied themselves with making blended oils and salves for the pharmacy as well as for Sage's shop. One afternoon, Sarah and Cherokee didn't have classes, so they came over to join them.

"What are we making today, Tessy?" Sarah asked as she popped one of Sage's favourite brownies in her mouth.

"Well, let's see… I was thinking one of my healing salves might be a good choice for today. Now, if you girls could go into the back kitchen and fetch my bin of beeswax, please, we will grate some and get started."

Tessy smiled with delight as she stood and watched the developing sisterhood. Here we are, a Crone and three Maidens working harmoniously on this blessed afternoon preparing these gifts from Mother Earth. She could not have been more content. She was definitely in her element and loving every minute. She began to wonder if she would soon be giving up a very large part of her life she had come to cherish. She knew in her heart of hearts that Marshall would never ask or expect her to change in any way. But would it just happen anyway? She hated these negative thoughts and shook them from her mind.

"My, girls. You've done a fine job. This salve has turned out just perfect. I couldn't have done a better job myself," she praised.

"Thanks," they chimed with pride.

"That was really fun and it's absolutely amazing how it all comes together," Sage added.

"Aye. Mother Nature knows exactly what she's doing," Tessy chuckled. "Now, let's have a nice cup of tea to celebrate."

The spring equinox was upon Ladyslipper, known as Ostara to Tessy. This, too, is a celebration of expectations and new beginnings, much the same as Imbolc. Only Ostara is a time of balance between the light and the dark, male and female energy, and the physical and spiritual worlds as well. It is all about the potential for growth, renewal and those new beginnings.

Sage was up early and gone to the shop. Tessy was happy to have the day to enjoy and pay homage to her Celtic holiday in her own solitary way.

She waited until the morning sun was at its highest, as she wanted to go outdoors to honour the season. With her she had three spring coloured candles, a soft green one to symbolize the blossoming earth, a bright yellow one to represent the sun, and one of lilac to honour the Divine. She also carried out a bowl of milk and a bowl of honey. She went into the greenhouse and selected three small pots and filled them with sand. She returned outside to her workstation and placed the pots on the table. She planted a candle in each pot, took three deep breaths, and quieted herself. She then began by lighting the candles and chanting:

I light this green candle for the earth to sprout and heal.
Next the yellow for the strength of the sun at this time of the wheel.
And now the lilac to honour the Divine as your love I truly feel.

She then took the bowl of milk and poured it into the bowl of honey, chanting:

This milk and honey I do gently combine
With thanks and gratitude for your sweet blessings so fine.
Please accept this offering, dear Earth, with my respect and love,
Just as the gifts you pour on me from all around and above.

She stirred the milk and honey until it was well mixed, then poured it on the ground and finished with,

This is my will, so mote it be.

Tessy stood very quiet with her eyes closed, breathing deeply and listening to the wonderful sounds of Mother Nature's spring awakening. Water was dripping from the buildings, and little birds happily chirped and sang sweet mating songs. She could hear a flock of Canada geese approaching with their perpetual honking. She looked up in time to see the massive, distinctive V in the sky, with one little fellow out of sync and trying his best to catch up and complete the perfect formation. Tessy laughed at Nature's humour. She stayed for quite some time, allowing the candles to burn down, then cleaned up and put the pots back in the greenhouse. During the remainder of the day, she prepared for her upcoming Easter celebration.

Tessy was up in the attic checking on how many baskets she had on hand for the children's Easter egg hunt, when she heard the front door slam and Sage loudly complaining about something. She hurried down and found Sage huffing and pacing around the kitchen.

"Sage, dear. What is the matter?"

"Sorry, Tessy. I didn't mean to slam the door so hard but I'm just so mad!"

"What happened, dear. Here. Come sit and tell me what's wrong."

"Well, I was just about to go back into the shop after picking up some supplies when this... this... woman came out of the insurance agency next door and accosted me!"

"Oh, my!" Tessy had been afraid this was going to happen. She knew Mrs. Chamberlain and her husband had been away on a cruise and had just returned so knew nothing of Sage or her shop until now.

"First, she asked me who I was and what I was doing going into my shop. Then she asked me what kind of shop I was opening. Well... I told her and she flipped out on me. She started calling me a witch and said Ladyslipper doesn't need or want any more of my kind. Then she said, 'We'll see about this!' And that she was going straight to the town office and have a talk with them."

"Oh, my!" Tessy repeated. "I'm sure they were glad to see her coming! Well, dear, don't you worry about her. That is Mrs. Chamberlain, and she and a couple of her society friends seem to think they can run the town, but as it turns out they are mostly just full of hot air and not taken too seriously."

"Yes! That was what she said her name was. How did you know?"

Tessy laughed heartily. "Oh, Sage, dear. She has been a slight irritation of mine for the past twenty five years or more and, unfortunately, I don't think that's going to change anytime soon."

24
A Grand Opening

The last ten days of March it was all hands on deck getting Sage's shop finished and ready for her grand opening April first. Most days Sage and Tommy were there from sunrise to sunset. Sarah and Cherokee stopped by every day after school, and even Matt, Brendon and Jason showed up on the weekend to help move in furniture.

Now all that was left to do was create the positive aura Sage desired for her shop – the smell, the sound, the feel. She had already purchased a diffuser to gently release the scent of essential oils. And one morning, on their way to the shop, Tessy and Sage stopped in to the Nurturing Nature to look for a small fountain to feature in her waiting area. It would be Sage's most lavish purchase, but she wanted to set the perfect ambiance for her clients. They chose a lovely one that ran soft and soothing. Sage smiled at Tessy, "Yes. This one. It will create just the right mood."

There was one more important element that Tessy felt Sage needed in her shop, so as a grand opening gift Tessy presented Sage with a large, gorgeous amethyst geode for the front office to absorb problems and release gentleness into the space. The aura in the room was inviting, relaxing and safe.

Tessy divided her time between the pharmacy and Sage's shop. She was in Sage's reception area sorting through a display box of their homemade massage oils when she heard the front door open. She turned to see Mrs. Chamberlain entering. She looked at Tessy and snorted. "I should have guessed you had a hand in all this. If any more of you people move to town, Ladyslipper will turn into the witch Salem of Canada."

"Aye. And look at the lesson in misjudgement we learned from all that."

"Humph!" exhaled the unimpressed intruder.

"What can we help ye with, Mrs. Chamberlain?"

"I just came by to let Ms. Haggerty know that I will be keeping an eye on her, and if I suspect any funny business whatsoever, I will be talking to the authorities, the health inspectors and anyone else I can think of."

Sage had come down from upstairs in time to hear Mrs. Chamberlain's warning, and stepped into the room.

"Well, Mrs. Chamberlain, I don't think you need be concerned. In fact, I invite you to be my first customer – on the house, of course."

"Oh sure! You'd like that, wouldn't you? Get me on one of your tables so you can perform some of your voodoo on me. Not a chance, young lady. Not a chance. Good day!" And she stormed out the door.

Tessy couldn't help by laugh. "Nicely done, my dear. I was a little concerned I might have to step in so she didn't trod all over ye, but I see now that you are more than capable of handling her all by yourself."

"Well, she may have caught me by surprise the other day, but I'm on to her now and will be sure to keep my guard up."

"Aye, probably a good idea to keep your shield of white light up. But just don't let her taint ye, dear. It's not worth it. Maybe between the pair of us we can, eventually, turn some of that venom she spews into honey!"

The first day of April arrived cloudy and cool, but the rain they had been forecasting was, thankfully, holding off. Sage and Tessy were in the kitchen finishing up their breakfast when there was a banging at the back door. Tessy opened it to find an anxious Tommy. Sage ran over to him.

"Tommy! What is it? What's the matter?"

"Oh, Sage! It's terrible!"

"What? What is?"

"I went down to the shop and the whole top floor has collapsed into the main floor."

"What? What are you talking about? What?" was all the frantic Sage kept saying as she fled around the kitchen.

All of a sudden Tommy starting laughing, "April fools!"

"Tommy! You bugger!" Sage couldn't believe he had just pulled such a horrible antic and playfully slapped him on the shoulder, stomping her feet. "How could you? I can't believe you did that!" She slapped him again.

Tessy, rather relieved herself, chuckled and added, "Tommy, that really was a wicked trick. You have to be careful startlin' an old girl like myself."

"Oh, come on, Tessy. You got to admit it was pretty funny. And you're the youngest middle-aged woman I know. You're going to outlast us all."

"Well, she's certainly going to outlast you if you ever pull a stunt like that again," Sage glared at him then smirked.

"Boy! I sure had you going. You should have seen the look on your face." Tommy buckled over with laughter.

"Stop laughing! It wasn't that funny."

"Okay. Okay. I'm sorry." Tommy reached for Sage and gave her a hug. "Are you ready to go and open your beautiful, well built, totally sound shop?"

The grand opening of The Healing Sage went very well, with maybe the exception of Mrs. Chamberlain, perched on a lawn chair outside her husband's neighbouring agency, glaring at Sage's potential clientele and taking account as to who was actually daring to enter. Just to be on the safe side, Tessy recited a simple chant to block any negativity from next door. As it turned out, however, most ignored Mrs. Chamberlain and her comments. This shop was quite a progressive step for Ladyslipper, and they couldn't wait to see what diverse types of therapy Sage had to offer.

25
Welcomed Kin

Within the first week, despite Mrs. Chamberlain's best efforts, Sage's little shop was doing well. Her massage therapy was especially busy, and even her Reiki sessions were booking up nicely. The Community Centre had already asked her to start some yoga classes a few evenings a week, and all in all, Sage was becoming a welcomed member of the community. She was in one of the back rooms when she heard the bell tinkle on the front door. When she came out to see who it was, tears sprang to her eyes. There stood her mother, Rosemary.

"Mom!" Sage ran to her mother and threw her arms around her and began crying.

"Hi, sweetheart." Her mother gently sighed, rocking her, stroking her hair, and dropping a few tears of her own.

"Mom, what are you doing here? Why didn't you let me know you were coming?"

"I wanted to surprise you."

"Well, you certainly accomplished that! How did you know where to find me?"

Her mother gave her an impish grin. "Tessy and I have been planning this for some time now."

"Tessy! Really?"

"Yes. As a matter of fact my bags are at her house right at the moment. She has graciously invited me to stay with her."

"Why don't you stay here with me?"

"Well, I'm very anxious to see the rest of your shop and your apartment, but I understand it is quite small and I don't want to get in your way."

"Yeah. It is. I guess we would be kinda tripping over one another. But if you decide you'd like to, that would be great too."

"Thank you, sweetheart, but Tessy insisted that I stay at Ashling Manor and that you are always welcome to come over whenever you wish. She is also anxious to go over our heritage. Isn't it exciting that we may be related?"

"I know! Make sure she tells you all about Liam and Maggie."

"Who?"

"Just get her to tell you the story. Then you'll understand."

Sage proudly gave her mom the tour of her shop and living space. They spent about an hour together, running over to Sheree's Café for a cup of coffee before Sage had to get back for an appointment. Her mom left after they made arrangements to meet at Ashling Manor later that evening for supper, at Tessy's request.

Tessy prepared a simple cabbage casserole, as she wasn't sure exactly what time Sage would be finished at the healing center. Shortly after 6 p.m. they were all seated in the living room enjoying a glass of wine and appetizers. The three ladies had a marvelous visit. Tessy repeated the short version of the Liam and Maggie story that Sage insisted she tell. And Tessy did acquire some helpful information from Rosemary regarding their past. She was looking forward to researching the details the next morning. There was an unfamiliar current running through the house that Tessy had not felt before, and she wanted to get to the bottom of it as soon as possible.

The ladies moved into the dining room to enjoy their meal and each other's company. Rosemary wanted to hear all about Tommy, and Sage was more than accommodating.

"Oh, Mom! You are going to just love him. He is so kind and funny and shy. He's finishing his mechanics course, working for Tessy's neighbour on the farm, and helped me redo my shop. He's amazing!"

"My. He sounds too good to be true."

"He is. And he's really cute, too!" Sage gushed.

Tessy laughed. "To be perfectly honest, Rosemary, I too think he is a fine young man, one very worthy of dating your daughter. He's very respectful and a hard worker. But I'm sure you will want to meet him yourself."

"Well, he does sound very nice and yes, I definitely am looking forward to meeting him. It's plain to see he certainly has captured my daughter's heart!"

"Grand. We'll have him over for Easter brunch this weekend and you two can get royally acquainted."

"Oh, Tessy! That would be awesome! Thank you." Sage got up and hugged Tessy's neck.

The evening continued on with comfortable conversation and laughter. Tessy went into the kitchen to get dessert and tea, returning to see Rosemary and Sage having a special moment, holding hands and smiling at one another. The love between mother and daughter was very apparent and truly wonderful to witness. The touching scene brought warmth to Tessy's heart and she thanked God. Rosemary and Sage looked up at Tessy; the moment was over but the warmth and the electric current remained. Tessy set the tray down on the table and handed out the dessert.

"Rosemary, would ye like a cup of tea with your parfait?"

"That would lovely, Tessy. Thank you."

The next morning Tessy was up early, and had completed her grounding, meditation and yoga routine before Rosemary made it downstairs. She had wanted to begin her research and decided to go in to the library and retrieve the photo albums Aunt Shannon had given her. She took them into the kitchen to look over while she had her coffee. Rosemary met her in the kitchen.

"Good morning, Tessy."

"Oh, morning to ye, Rosemary. Help yourself to some coffee. Did ye sleep well?"

"Yes, thank you. You have such a lovely home, Tessy."

"Well, thank ye. I've never tired of it. My Dermot and I had many wonderful years here together. It would have been nice to fill it with children but we were never blessed with them. So I invite children over as often as possible," she chuckled.

"Sage mentioned that you have many celebrations here. How wonderful."

"Aye. As a matter of fact, you'll be here for what I like to call my Easter egg-stravaganza!"

"Terrific! I would love to help in any way I can." Rosemary picked up her cup, stepped over to the counter, and poured herself a coffee. She stopped behind Tessy on her way back to the table to lean in and take a look at the photos she was presently pondering over.

"These are some of my relatives from Ireland," Tessy offered. "I haven't seen many of them in a long while and some I didn't know at all until my Auntie helped me out. I've now documented their names and which picture they belong to in order to keep a detailed account."

Tessy slowly turned a few pages when all of a sudden Rosemary gasped and all but yelled, "Stop! Wait! Don't turn the page. I know that picture! My grandfather had that exact same picture in a frame for years."

Tessy was stunned. "Which picture? Which one?"

"This one. Right here on the left," she pointed. "That is my grandfather when he was a young boy. He's the one standing closest to the horse. It was the last picture he had taken with his horse before they left to settle in Canada. It broke his heart to leave that animal. I remember him telling me her name was Molly."

"Well, that's my Uncle Jim."

"Yes. James Haggerty. My grandfather. We are related! Oh, Tessy. How exciting. I can't wait to tell Sage. She'll be thrilled!"

"Well. Imagine that. A long lost cousin, ye are."

The two ladies hugged as their bond had just become stronger. Finding a new relative was an exhilarating experience for them both. They began flipping through the album to see if there were any other coincidental photos. Even though Tessy knew there are no coincidences – it all happens for a reason.

Rosemary couldn't wait to get dressed and run down to Sage's shop to tell her the good news.

Sage was at the front desk when Rosemary burst in the front door. "Mom! What is it? What's wrong?"

"Oh, sorry. Nothing. Everything is great. Guess what? We're related."

"Of course we're related. You're my mother."

Rosemary laughed. "No, silly. We're related to Tessy!"

"What? Really! That's great. How… why… what do you mean?"

"Grandpa Jim is Tessy's uncle! Can you believe that?"

"Great Grandpa Jim! Really? That's awesome! How did you two figure that out?"

"We were looking at photos this morning, and remember that picture of Grandpa and his horse Molly? Well, Tessy has that very same picture. And there it was. I couldn't believe my eyes."

"I'm in shock! I mean, what are the chances? And, what are the chances that I would decide to move to Saskatchewan, find Ladyslipper, set up a shop, and discover we are related to this amazing person who lives here?"

The news spread throughout Ladyslipper like wildfire! Before long, everyone was buzzing about Tessy's new relatives. Mrs. Chamberlain, especially, was all abuzz! She had her two constant cohorts, Mrs. Mason and Mrs. Wright, over for tea to assess the situation and see how it could best be handled.

"We cannot have any more of these witches moving in to town. Before long they will just take over and we will all be under their spell. I mean look at what has happened already with all their hocus-pocus. The two of them are making up and selling all sorts of potions and lotions and people are just slathering themselves with God only knows what! And that young witch is waving her hands over people and supposedly healing them with divine energy. Have you ever heard of such hogwash?"

Mrs. Wright and Mrs. Mason knew better than to actually answer the question, as they knew there was only one true answer and that was whatever Mrs. Chamberlain decided it was. She was definitely on one of her rants so they politely nodded and sipped their tea in silence.

Tessy, herself, couldn't wait to call Marshall and let him know about her exciting discovery. She was just about to hang up on the fifth ring when Dotty puffed into the phone.

"Hello. Tayse residence."

"Dotty, dear. It's Tessy. Where did I get ye from?"

"Tessy. Hi. Oh, just running in from doing a few errands. Bert and I were hauling in groceries from the car when I heard it ringing. How are you doing?"

"Grand. Just grand. You and Bert are doing well, I trust?"

"Yes. Couldn't be better."

"Good. Glad to hear it. I'm assuming the good doctor is not about, then?"

"No. Sorry. He's out but I can sure get him to give you a call when he gets in."

"That would be wonderful. Thanks Dotty. I have some very exciting news I can't wait to share with you all."

"Oh. Sounds intriguing. Best not tell me before Dr. Tayse gets in though. I cannot keep a secret to save my life, and I'm sure he'd rather hear it from you instead of me."

Tessy chuckled. "All right then. I'll wait for him to call me back. Thanks, Dotty. Take care and say hi to Bert for me."

"Oh Tessy, before you go. Did you get my e-mail about the hors d'oeuvres we were talking about for the wedding?"

"Yes. Thank you, Dotty. I did get it but I haven't had a chance to sit down and really go over it. I should have some time this week and then I'll give you a call."

"Great. Talk to you then. Bye for now, Tessy."

"Bye-bye, Dotty, dear."

An hour later Marshall called and was as shocked and elated as Tessy to hear the news.

"Well, sounds like our guest list might be growing," he laughed.

"Aye. I hadn't even thought of that, love. Good point. What do ye think? Would ye mind if we sent an invitation to Rosemary and her children? I'm not sure they could attend coming all the way from Ontario, but it would be nice to at least invite them."

"Not at all, sweetheart. Of course we should invite them. They are family."

"Marshall, dear, thank you for being so understanding. How did I become so blessed to have such a wonderful rogue as yourself in my life?"

Marshall laughed. "Just lucky, I guess. You can show me your appreciation next time we're together."

"Oh! You cheeky man! What am I going to do with you?"

"Again, I have a suggestion or two," Marshall quipped.

"Stop that right now and behave yourself!" Tessy blushed.

Marshall just laughed.

"Now, on a more serious note, love. I finished mailing out all the wedding invitations today. Should ye think of anyone else you'd like to invite I do have a few left."

"That's wonderful, sweetheart. No, I can't think of anyone just off hand, but I will let you know as soon as possible if I do. Wow, I guess this makes it pretty official then, doesn't it? No backing out now."

"Nye. Ye've still got a good six weeks or so for ye to be changin' your mind," teased Tessy.

They lovingly teased for a few minutes more, then said goodnight. Tessy hung up and scolded herself for ever having had negative thoughts about marrying such an amazing man. She would check herself on that from now on.

26

Great Extravaganzas

Tessy's Easter egg-stravaganza is always held on Good Friday. It is a fun way to start the long weekend yet still allows people to have the remaining few days set aside for family. There are usually fewer in attendance than her Christmas in July celebration; this year there were about twenty children confirmed for the hunt. It was another event that Tessy loved to host. Her only disappointment was that Marshall was on call this weekend and could not join in the festivities. However, on a good note, this was the weekend that Marshall's son Kyle was arriving home from Africa and would be there to celebrate Easter with him.

Sarah, Cherokee, Sage and Tommy volunteered to hide the Easter eggs while Tessy and Rosemary prepared a light brunch of deviled eggs, an assortment of salads, cold ham, croissants and a fruit tray. Sarah came in with her basket finally empty. "Boy, it's not easy finding hiding spots for that many Easter eggs. Even in your yard, Tessy!"

Tessy chuckled. "Well each little one gets ten eggs so with the numbers that we have, two hundred should work out nicely. Did ye find some dandy spots for the older children to hunt down?"

"Yeah. I think it will take them a while to find the more difficult ones."

"Grand. I like to make it a bit of a challenge for the older children. They seem to have more fun with it that way."

The Easter egg hunt was scheduled for 11 a.m. sharp. At 10:50 a.m. the children, including Emma and Becky, were in their brightly coloured rubber boots and rain jackets all lined up in the back yard intently listening to Tessy's instructions.

"Now, ye know when ye come to my house that we use our manners, right?"

The children all chimed, "Yes."

"Good. So we'll have no pushing or shoving. In fact, it would be nice if ye helped your friend find their eggs if they're havin' trouble, right?"

Again, "Yes," chorused through the air.

"Good. Now, the Easter Bunny and I had a wee chat this mornin' and I was told that to eliminate any hurt feelings, each child, young or old, is allowed ten eggs. No more, no less. Sarah and Cherokee will hand you your baskets. Now, the wee children will have a head start of five minutes, then the older children may join in. It would be awfully nice and greatly appreciated if you older children would help out any wee child that is having difficulty first, before filling your own basket. There's plenty to go around. Okay, so are we ready to go hunt for eggs?"

"Yes!" the children shouted as they jumped up and down.

"Way ye go, then." Tessy chuckled as she stepped out of the way so as not to get trampled.

Twenty-five minutes later every nook and cranny had been searched, the baskets were full, and the children were satisfied with their treasure. Everyone stayed to sample the brunch, with some of the parents even managing to persuade their offspring to eat something besides chocolate eggs.

By 1:30 p.m. everyone was gone, and the cleanup crew were busy in the kitchen. Tessy was washing and the girls were drying.

"Tessy, do you ever get tired of having these parties?" Sarah actually shocked herself by asking that question out loud and added, "Sorry. I didn't mean that you should be or anything. They are always amazing and everything… I, I just meant…" She was now stammering.

"Sarah!" Cherokee blurted, staring wide-eyed at her friend, not quite able to believe her ears.

Tessy laughed. "It's okay, dears. No need to apologize. I suppose to some it might seem a bit odd or eccentric, but remember I had no children to spoil with birthday parties or, up until now, any family close by to enjoy the holidays with. The community of Ladyslipper is my family and I take pleasure in hosting these events for them."

"That's so nice. I'm sorry. I guess I've never thought of it that way. I am so glad you are now a part of our family. We love you very much." Sarah dropped her dishtowel down on the counter and wrapped her arms around Tessy.

"Thank you, sweetheart. I love all of you as well." Tessy had to stop, dry her hands, and dab her eyes and nose with her hankie.

"Okay, but this doesn't mean you are going to give up your Ladyslipper family, does it?" Cherokee was getting concerned that she might, eventually, be left out.

"Not on your life, dear. Once family, always family." Tessy pulled her in for a group hug.

Sage, Tommy and Rosemary had left after the brunch so Rosemary and Tommy could spend some time getting to know one another. Rosemary was leaving tomorrow so she could celebrate part of the long weekend with Rowan and Saffron as well.

"Ahh, Mom, it's been such a short visit. I wish you didn't have to go."

"I know, honey. I wish so, too. Next time I will come for a longer visit, I promise. Maybe I can swing it sometime this summer."

"That would be awesome. Maybe Saffron could come then, too." Sage was feeling brighter.

"That would be wonderful, wouldn't it?" Rosemary agreed.

"Well, it was sure nice meeting you Mrs. Haggerty," Tommy bashfully intervened.

"Thank you, Tommy… but it's Ms. Haggerty or Rosemary. It was a pleasure meeting you, as well. I feel quite confident about my Sage dating you. To be perfectly honest, I wasn't sure at first. But now that we've had some time together, I'm okay with it."

"Whuff… that's a relief!" Tommy swiped at his forehead.

Rosemary and Sage just laughed.

Early the next morning Rosemary, after a tearful parting, was packed into her rental vehicle and on her way to the airport. Tessy invited the teary-eyed Sage in for a cup of tea and some sympathetic conversation.

"Oh, Tessy, I miss her so much already," Sage sniffed before she blew her nose one more time.

"I know, Sage dear. It's always hard to say goodbye to a loved one. But isn't it nice to know there are no boundaries or borders on love? It travels with ye wherever you are. Your mam has left her love here and she took yours to go."

Sage lifted her head and smiled. She loved Tessy's way of putting things. So simple and down to earth you wondered why you didn't think of it yourself. In the short time she had come to know this wise woman, she knew she would aspire to be just like her and learn whatever wisdom she had to offer.

"Thanks, Tessy. You're right. I needed that," was all she said as she accepted her cup from Tessy. Sage replayed the wise woman's words many times over during the weeks that followed.

The last Saturday of April, the town of Ladyslipper scheduled an Environmental Awareness Day and community clean up in conjunction with an environmental program Tessy had launched last fall called the Gorgeous Garbage Drive. She had presented it to both the Town Council and the schools, and with the exception of Mrs. Chamberlain's best efforts to squash it, it was received with great enthusiasm. The schools had adopted the program into their curriculum. The town adopted it into their hearts. They were now ready to put all their hard work into action. The students were especially anxious to see their efforts set in motion. The art classes had their garbage bins brightly painted, the trades department had the cleverly designed receptacles ready to be put in place, the home economics classes were eager to set up some tables and sell their homemade cloth grocery bags, all-natural environmentally friendly cleaning products, and baking. Yes, the fruits of the town's labour were about to be enjoyed.

Ladyslipper had what the kids called an awesome makeover. By the end of the afternoon, it looked lovely. The receptacles were attractive and sturdy with their bins furbished cheery and colourful. The kids had a successful sale, selling plenty of cloth grocery bags, baking and natural products. The street sweeper was out all day and the boulevards and ditches were raked clean. Yes, it was quite a makeover extravaganza.

27
Spring Merriment and May Poles

It was a beautiful Sunday morning. The sun was warm, the birds were singing, and the dragonflies were flitting. Tessy was out in her garden just finishing the final touches of starting up the waterfall into her pond. She walked over to the shed and plugged it in to the outdoor electrical outlet. It took a minute, then all of a sudden the sound of trickling water was echoed off the shrubs and encased the back yard.

Tessy smiled with delight. She was so captured by the beauty of the day that she decided to take a long walk out into the pasture behind her grove of trees. It used to be part of the property at one time, but had long since been split off and now belonged to her neighbour, Danny Baker. She knew he wouldn't mind and that he hadn't moved his cattle over there yet this season. She wandered for about an hour out among the sweet grasses and wild flowers that were peeking through. She even found clusters of lovely crocuses that cheerfully greeted her. She had roamed quite a distance when she decided to head back. She maneuvered her way through a barbed wire fence and was headed down the footpath towards her house when she saw two of the society ladies, Mrs. Mason and Mrs. Wright, approaching her. They stopped and blocked her way.

"We noticed you missed Sunday service again this morning," sniffed one of the women.

Tessy smiled. "Not at all. I'm sure it was lovely, but I was just at a much larger service."

The ladies were shocked with this answer. Mrs. Wright asked, "Where would that be?"

"Well, I took a walk out into the meadow, looked up to the Universe, and there was the good Lord himself standing at the pulpit with His arms stretched out wide with love. I took a look around at the congregation of sweet grasses, field daisies, yarrow and chamomile swaying to the tunes of a choir of songbirds and bumblebees. We all prayed and gave thanks for our blessings. 'Twas such a beautiful service, 'twas. Too bad ye missed it!" And with that she gave them a farewell nod and carried on her way.

Tessy's next festivity is May Day, or dating back to ancient Celtic heritage, Beltane. It is a festival that centers on the energy that appears as the spring season fully emerges. It is a time of soaking in the warmth, picking blossoming flowers, and the awaking of our senses for others. It is a time of community to gather friends and neighbours together; therefore, this is the one occasion Tessy encourages guests to contribute by bringing a favourite dish of their own to share. This year Tessy's ethnic contribution was a crockery of fish soup, and a baked caramel custard.

The theme Tessy spun on this year's celebration was Medieval Games, which surprisingly were not that different from the outdoor games played today. They included tug o' war, ring toss, walking on stilts, blindfold games, and horseshoes, and she snuck in a piñata for the small children.

Of course, there was the most popular and common tradition of May Day, that of dancing around the Maypole. Originally, it was a way to assure fertility of the land and its people. Tessy has a specific pole she uses from year to year and has a spot in the back yard that was designated just for this occasion. She starts with a four-inch thick pole twelve feet long, and twelve-foot lengths of ribbon in a rainbow of colours. Before she puts it up, she drives a long nail through all the ribbons that have been re-enforced at the end with duct tape on each side. She doesn't drive the nail all the way in, though; she leaves a bit of a gap between the nail head and the pole for ease of movement as well as for securing a decorative foam wreath covered with silk flowers and greenery. Each year, the pole is erected in the permanent concrete hole she and Dermot had devised years earlier. When it is not in use, a large stepping-stone covers it, and a birdbath perches on top of the stone

This year, she asked Tommy over to help erect the pole. The children came over days ahead to help set up the games and construct make-shift tables made from sawhorses and sheets of plywood to hold all the food. Tommy secured them with a couple of screws to ensure they would be more stable while in use. Matt, Brendon and Jason were put in charge of all the stilts events. They had more fun goofing around on them than doing any planning, until Tessy came along with one of her lists and coached them as to what was to happen. Sage was to oversee the blindfold game, Tommy was in charge of the horseshoe tournament, Cherokee took tug o' war, and Sarah was on ring toss and piñata duty. Tessy would move around to each of the games so everyone could have a chance to go and participate in whatever event they would like to join in. Dancing around the Maypole would be left until closer to the end of the day.

Guests would begin arriving at noon to set out their culinary offerings, so Tessy went upstairs at eleven to get ready. This year the weather was cooperating. There had been past years when they danced around the May Pole with snow on the ground. Tessy decided to wear her lovely cotton dress, covered with tiny pink flowers. It was loose and comfortable and she did enjoy wearing it.

Soon there was a multitude of ethnic dishes arriving, each one looking as delicious as the next. The yard was filling up and the games commenced. The afternoon was filled with fun, frolic and merriment. Tessy was leaning up against her majestic maple enjoying the laughter when she noticed something moving in the back bushes. She carefully crept up along the edge of the hedge and slipped in behind. She almost laughed out loud when she saw the sight. It was Mrs. Chamberlain leaning through the bushes, as far as she dared, trying to see what was going on. Tessy cleared her throat. Mrs. Chamberlain stumbled back.

"Good afternoon, Mrs. Chamberlain," Tessy said, disguising her giggle. "Lovely day, isn't it? Would ye care to come in and join us?"

"Why on earth would I do that? Of course not!" Mrs. Chamberlain offered, straightening her dress. "I… I… I was walking past and just wondering what all the commotion was about. You really should be a little more considerate of your neighbours, Ms. McGuigan," she continued as she started to march past Tessy.

"All of my neighbours are in attendance but, thank ye, I'll keep that in mind, Mrs. Chamberlain."

"I should think so. Good day," Mrs. Chamberlain huffed, as she straightened her dress again, raised her chin high into the air and carried on.

"Good day, Mrs. Chamberlain."

Tessy chuckled all the way back to the house.

The rest of the day sailed by without incident. It was near time to start the dance around the Maypole. There were two dances with appropriate music set for each, one for the children and one for the young maidens. The children were first, of course. After some organization and Tessy leading the way they merrily followed her like the pied piper, giggling, skipping and laughing. Parents took pictures and everyone smiled and clapped with delight at the sight. After their procession was finished the ribbons were untangled and the true ceremonious Maypole dance was arranged with all maidens, thirteen and over, to gather around. They each took a ribbon and waited for Tessy to start the music and announce for them to proceed. They looked lovely. Most had silk flower wreaths in their hair and were daintily dressed. Tessy smiled, hit PLAY on the CD player, and nodded for them to begin.

As the young men stood watching the lasses, with stars of anticipation in their eyes, Tessy stood observing their reactions. When Matt watched his female classmates dance he saw them in a light he had never noticed before. He was almost mesmerized and caught himself smiling. Suddenly he shook back to consciousness and jokingly bumped up against Brendon, who was also in a slight trance. Tessy witnessed and grinned. She was elated that the Maypole was still performing its appointed role after all these centuries.

The day was coming to a close. People were gathering their leftovers and hunting Tessy down to thank her and say goodbye. Tessy graciously bade farewell to one and all. A small group of ladies stayed behind to help with the cleanup. Soon all the dishes were done and the kitchen was in order once again. The children were coming back tomorrow to help with the yard clean up.

It had been a long day and Tessy was feeling it. She was glad to have this time alone to celebrate the remaining Beltane in solitary. On the wheel of the year, Beltane sits directly opposite another major holiday for Tessy, Samhain. Both festivals are traditionally celebrated by bonfires. She had prepared for this bonfire days before, making sure the kindling and wood were stacked just so in order for it to ignite with ease. She would wait for darkness to near before striking the match. At Samhain, the veil between our world and the spirit world is open; at Beltane, it is the veil between our world and the fae that is open. Beltane is the time when faeries surface and begin spreading their magick throughout the gardens.

Earlier in the week she had purchased some used, clean baby food jars at the thrift store and fastened light-weight wire around the necks of the jars so they would hang nicely in her trees. She placed tea lights in them and began lighting them as she hung them in the lower branches.

Just as darkness was approaching, she went to the green house to retrieve some tulip and lily bulbs and a Lady's Mantle shrub. She took them to a cleared garden patch and began to plant them. As she placed them into the ground she chanted:

These gifts from Mother Earth I plant with love.
I entrust them to the fae as Flora watches from above.
The Green Man will smile when they flourish and shine
In their brilliant colours so vibrant and fine.
So now I do ask for them to thrive and thrill me
As this is my will – so mote it be.

When she was done, she lit the bonfire and danced around and around inviting all the faeries to join her and to flit from tea light to tea light. Aye, the spring season was now in full stride and the gardens were filled with magick.

28
Dreaded Dreams Come True

A week or so after Beltane, Tessy awoke with an unusual uneasiness. Before she went to bed last night she had noticed a soft glowing ring around the moon, and this was the third night in a row that dreams of the ocean with smoke or fog wafting over it crept into her conscious. These were bad signs all around. Aye, there was a deep emotional storm coming and the smoky fog kept her from seeing what it was.

She untangled herself out from under the covers and plunked her feet on the floor. Merlin had come in and was staring at her.

"Aye, I agree. It looks like I've been wrestling with a bear all night and 'tis not far from the truth. You can feel the storm, too, can't ye, wee one?"

Tessy had just finished cleaning up the kitchen after breakfast. Her murky aura had not lifted, so she decided to head out to the gardens to see if that would help her mood, when the phone rang. She froze. She knew it was bad news. She slowly answered it on the third ring.

"Hello," was her uncharacteristic greeting.

"Tess?"

"Aye."

"Oh Tessy! This is cousin Lizzy."

Tessy immediately knew what the bad news was and dreaded hearing it. Lizzy was Auntie Shannon's oldest daughter.

"Oh Tessy!" Lizzy repeated. "Mom's gone. She passed early this morning," then she broke down.

"Lizzy, dear, I'm so sorry," and Tessy too started to weep. "Bless her soul. She was such a lovely lady."

The two spent some time consoling one another before hanging up, with Lizzy reassuring Tessy someone would call soon with the arrangement details.

Tessy sat at the kitchen table with memories of Aunt Shannon running through her. The beautiful woman was her godmother, the woman her mother had entrusted to raise her and Keenan. All of a sudden she gasped, "Keenan!" She would need to call him immediately. She picked up the phone and dialed the numbers. There was a busy signal. She re-dialed a few minutes later and Keenan answered on the first ring.

"Oh Keenan, dear!"

"Aye, Tessy, I know. I've just heard. Cousin Richard called." Richard was Lizzy's brother.

Tessy started to cry.

"Now there, Tess, don't cry. Auntie lived a good fair life. 'Twas her time, 'twas."

"I know, Keenan. But ye're just never ready even when ye know the time has come."

"Aye, 'tis true. Well, I guess I'll be comin' over the pond a mite earlier than expected."

"Ye're comin' then, Keenan?"

"Aye, of course. Wouldn't miss the proper sending off of the grand old gal."

"But the wedding is just a month away. Will ye be able to come again, then?"

"Well, this hasn't given us much time to do any plannin', but what would ye say to havin' a houseguest for the next month?"

"Oh Keenan! Really? That would be grand. I'd love for ye to come stay for the month."

"Grand. Well, it's settled then. I'll make some calls to see what I can arrange."

"Will Mary be joinin' ye?"

"Nye. She'll be coming over closer to the wedding. That way we only have to cancel one of the flights we've already booked."

"Aye, of course, dear."

"Well, I'd better go if I'm to be arrangin' some new flights, then."

"Aye. And Keenan, don't be forgettin' your wee parcel that Auntie had sent ye."

"Not to worry. Wouldn't dream of leavin' it behind. Curiosity has definitely captured this cat!"

Tessy chuckled. "Grand. See you soon, dear brother. Give my love to your Mary and the rest."

"Aye, Tess. Bye for now."

Tessy was feeling better already. Her twin was going to be here in just a few short days. He, of course, would be flying in to Winnipeg as that is where the funeral would be held, but then he'd be returning with Tessy to Ashling Manor. That is where they would open the little parcels, which would, hopefully, reveal this longstanding mystery.

The next phone call was to Marshall.

"Well, you and Keenan will be staying here with us. Not another word about it!" Marshall insisted when Tessy first suggested that she and Keenan stay in a hotel.

"Are ye sure, love? That's a lot of extra work for Dotty, and with Kyle having just returned from Africa we don't want to put anyone out."

"Of course I'm sure. Dotty would be insulted if you did anything else, and Kyle is looking forward to spending some time with you. I just won't hear of you not staying with us."

"Well, thank ye, love. We truly appreciate it. It will be nice to have ye near at this difficult time. I'm so glad you and Auntie had a chance to meet. She thought ye a real catch, ye know?"

Marshall laughed. "It was definitely an honour to know her. And I'm glad I had the chance to tell her the stories of you she shared would not go to waste."

"Ye just never mind with your nonsense, now."

When Tessy told Sage that one of her relatives had passed away, she was extremely sad. Even though they had never met, she had come to know her through Tessy's stories. She was unable to accompany Tessy to Winnipeg due to scheduled appointments, though she truly would have liked to.

Tessy decided to drive to Winnipeg, as that way Keenan wouldn't have to purchase another plane ticket from there to Regina. This would also give them plenty of time to royally catch up on the long drive to Ladyslipper.

Between the Tuckers, Sage, and Tommy, she could leave and not have one concern about her animals or Ashling Manor. As she was travelling down the highway she knew she was so very blessed to have such wonderful friends. Then she realized they were actually now family except for Tommy and, who knew, maybe that would change with time as well. She smiled at the thought as the prairie scenery flashed past her. Without Sarah and Cherokee to keep her company, the drive seemed a bit longer than the last time she travelled it.

It had certainly felt like a full day when she pulled into Marshall's driveway. She shut the engine off and just sat for a moment. When she looked up at the house, there was Marshall standing at the open door. His smile was broad and full of tenderness. She smiled back at him as he made his way down the steps towards her. He opened her door and gathered her up in his arms as she crawled out.

Tessy and Marshall would have a couple of days together before Keenan was scheduled to arrive. Tessy spent one of those days over at Auntie Shannon's with her cousins. They insisted that she join them to sort through her things to see what she might like. They were a close family, with Tessy and Keenan treated as siblings.

After such an emotional day of sorting through boxes of memories, Tessy laid quiet in bed listening to Marshall's deep breathing which was just a hint away from a soft snore. Keenan was landing tomorrow in the early afternoon and they were meeting him at the airport. This, too, would be an emotional day but one she was very much looking forward to.

29
The Greeting of Keenan O'Connor

As Tessy and Marshall waited patiently at the arrival gate for Keenan, they amused themselves by people watching. They made up little tales of where they came from and why they were landing in Winnipeg. There were people from every walk of life in every size and colour imaginable. It was quite enjoyable.

Finally, Keenan's flight number and city of origin was announced. Tessy's heart skipped a beat, then quickened. They stepped a little closer to the escalator to watch for him. They observed, one by one, passengers carefully maneuvering onto the moving steps, luggage and backpacks of all kinds in hand. Tessy caught a glimpse of who she thought might be Keenan close to the top, but there was such a crowd in the way she couldn't be certain. All of sudden, there he was smiling that devilish smile, eyes twinkling and looking as wonderful as she remembered.

"Keenan! Keenan, dear!" Tessy called out, wildly waving her arms.

"Well, there she is, then. Me older sister, herself," Keenan returned as they wrapped their arms around one another.

"Now, don't be startin' any of your blarney, right off," she laughed while dabbing her wet eyes with a hankie. "Nine minutes does not an older sister make."

"Well, all I know is what I was told… that ye arrived hollering your lungs out before I popped along," Keenan laughed.

Marshall stood back smiling, enjoying the bantering between the siblings. When he spotted Keenan, he would have easily picked him out in a crowd as Tessy's brother. Right away he recognized their similar features. He was not much taller than Tessy, his reddish curly hair flipping up around his Irish cap, a round button nose and, of course, that smile with those large, dancing, green Irish eyes. Yep, definitely Tessy's twin!

Tessy and Keenan turned toward Marshall simultaneously.

"Keenan, this is Marshall Tayse. Marshall, my brother, Keenan O'Connor."

They stretched out their hands, firmly grasped, and shook. Marshall immediately realized that Keenan was a man of hard work. He was extremely fit; his hands were strong and callused yet conveyed an air of easiness. Marshall instantly liked him.

"Well now, so you're the fine rogue that's caught my sister's eye." Then he leaned in closer and added, "I'll have ye know you're takin' on quite a challenge. But don't mind, I'm here to talk ye through it."

Marshall heartily laughed.

"Keenan, I swear, I'll march ye right back up those stairs and plunk ye back on that plane if ye don't behave," Tessy scolded.

Keenan just shrugged his shoulders, smiled a broad smile, winked at Marshall and said, "I'm starving. Where's there a pub that we can go get a bite and raise a pint or two in honour of our dear old Auntie Shannon?"

An hour later they were comfortably seated at the Olde Emerald Stone.

"Dandy spot, this," Keenan announced, looking around and seemingly being pleasantly surprised. "But the proof is in the puddin' they say, or in this case, steak and kidney pie and a pint."

Marshall laughed. He was enjoying this character immensely. Everything he came up with proved to be entertaining.

They each ordered a pint, and when the server left the table Keenan raised his glass high and recited, "Death leaves a heartache no one can heal; Love leaves a memory no one can steal. To Auntie Shannon... God bless ye, dear. Sláinte."

They each raised their glasses and took a generous gulp.

Tessy smiled at her brother. "That was very nice, Keenan. Knowing ye, I was expecting more the old, May your glass be ever full, may the roof over your head be always strong, and may ye be in heaven half an hour before the devil knows you're dead."

Keenan looked at her with shock, "I'm crushed ye'd think such a thing!" Then he laughed and said, "Truth be told, 'twas on the tip of me tongue, but I thought better of it."

Everyone laughed.

They finished up their lunch and headed back to Marshall's to get Keenan settled in. Introductions were made, and it was evident that even under these heartbreaking circumstances, it was going to be an enjoyable visit.

Marshall was in his home office on a conference call, so Tessy and Keenan decided to stretch their legs and go for a walk. Tessy linked her arm into her brother's as they strolled along the beautifully manicured Wellington Crescent.

"Oh, Keenan, dear, it's so nice to have ye near. I miss ye something terrible."

"Aye, Tessy, 'tis grand to see ye, too. However, ye may not be saying that after havin' me under foot for a whole month," he chuckled, patting her hand.

"No fear of that – even with all your blarney."

Keenan just gave his sister a devilish smile and they walked in silence for a few moments.

"Tess, when we get back to that mansion your fella' calls a house, do ye think we should go ahead and open my wee parcel?"

"No! Not on your life. That is the very reason I did not bring mine. I believe Auntie said for us to be alone together when we opened them. Therefore, that should be when we get to Ashling Manor and not before."

"Aye. I suppose," Keenan grumbled. "But it's been 'bout drivin' me mad!"

Tessy just laughed and nudged up against her brother.

30
A Grand Farewell to a Fine Lady

The morning of the funeral Tessy was up early, even before Dotty. She wanted to watch the sun rise on this sad day, to embed it in her memory much like she did the day she laid her beloved Dermot to rest. She went out into the garden to feel nature encompass her. She placed her hand gently on an oak tree and felt it lovingly comfort her. "Oh, mighty oak, thank ye for your strength."

Spotting a hawthorn tree just starting to come into bloom, she walked over and stood under it looking up into the bursting branches, quieted into meditation and asked the hawthorn's permission to pick some baby blossoms to carry in a sachet to help with her sadness today. She dug into her housecoat pocket and pulled out a rose quartz crystal and placed it at the base of the tree as a gift of appreciation. She took off her slippers, stepped onto the dew-covered grass, and let her feet soak up the great Mother's fresh, cool moisture. With the warmth of the morning sun on her face and the dampness seeping in to her toes, she allowed herself to quietly weep. Other than Keenan, this was the last of her close living relatives, and today they would give her ashes back to the earth.

The sound of a door closing brought Tessy back to reality. From behind the bushes she could see Dotty coming across the yard heading to the main house. Tessy looked up and saw a robin perched in the hawthorn. "Well, I guess this sad day has begun, then." Then she slowly made her way back into the house to help Dotty in the kitchen.

Hours later, with everyone dressed in their Sunday best, Marshall stood at the door holding it open as they all descended down the steps and into the large limo. Tessy had enjoyed her limo rides; however, today's trip was one she was not looking forward to.

Due to Auntie Shannon having lived in Canada so long, combined with the fact that her children did not observe the true Irish way, she had more of a Canadian traditional service. It did; however, on the insistence of Tessy and Keenan, include the marching and playing of the bagpipes. They also insisted on hosting the wake that followed. They were not about to have Auntie Shannon forgotten any time soon! It would be the life celebration of the fine lady she was. They had booked the back room of the Olde Emerald Stone with plenty of music, food, stout and Irish whiskey. Keenan was never without an Irish quote, nor a whiskey to go with it. Tessy told Marshall, Dotty and Bert to "Come on in and hang on tight… t'will prove to be quite a ride!" And that it was. There were many friends and relations who remembered the old days and were more than happy to share their tales and respect for the lovely old Irish lass. With Keenan at the helm, they sang all the old Irish tunes and raised their glasses, and the more they raised their glasses the louder the tunes and wilder the tales.

The celebration went on into the evening with people, eventually, paying their last respects to the family and trailing off home. With only Keenan and a few of the die-hards left, Tessy, Marshall, Dotty and Bert were ready to leave. Tessy knew getting Keenan out of there was going to be next to impossible. She figured he would put up less of a fight if Marshall went over to try and convince him.

"He won't hit me will he? You Irish do have a reputation, you know." Marshall gulped.

"Well, now, pretty much anything is possible, at this stage," Tessy honestly answered.

"Great! Thanks!" Marshall stared at her.

"Well, we'll need a wee bit of strategy behind this. I'll go and see if the manager will come in and announce the time is up. Maybe that would help?"

"Well, it won't hurt. Better than me having some teeth knocked out."

Tessy chuckled as she ran off to find the manager and possibly a bouncer. Keenan wasn't very big but he was pretty mighty, especially after a bucket full of whiskey. It wouldn't be the first time she'd seen him in a brawl. Sober, he is the most gentle, happy-go-lucky fellow you'd ever want to meet. Drunk… well, that would be another story. Feisty little bugger!

Apparently, this wasn't the first time the manager had encountered this problem. With a very large bouncer behind him he bellied up to the bar where Keenan was leaning, put his arm around Keenan, and jovially joked and talked with him for a few minutes. Before you knew it, they were best buddies and walking arm in arm out to the limo. He poured Keenan in to the backseat and they were off.

"Phew… That went better than expected," Tessy sighed.

"I'll say. Especially for me!" Marshall agreed.

"Aye. But we did celebrate Auntie's passing in grand Celtic style, didn't we!" Tessy giggled into Marshall's shoulder.

31
Disguises, Mystery and Intrigue

Sage locked Tessy's door and skipped down the front steps. It had been her turn to check on the animals and now she was headed off to her shop. As she merrily strolled along the footpath towards town, she wondered how Tessy was making out. She was sorry she had been unable to accompany Tessy to show the love, support and respect she felt for her. Tessy meant the world to Sage and she would have liked to show her just how much.

Trekking along the cracked sidewalks of Ladyslipper, she played the childhood game of "Step on a crack break your mothers back." She pondered as to where such a cruel nursery rhyme originated. She would ask Tessy; if anyone knew, it would be her.

She was in the shop about half an hour when she heard the bell on the door tinkle. She looked up to witness a woman rushing in wearing large, dark sunglasses, a hat pulled down as far as it would go, and a trench coat with the collar up. Sage, sporting a puzzled smirk, watched her as she dodged and snuck past the front windows. It reminded her of a scene in a really bad movie!

"Can I help you?" Sage finally asked, hoping the giggle in her had not surfaced.

"Yes," whispered the woman. "I would like to book a massage and possibly one of those raking things people have been talking about. You wouldn't have an available appointment this morning, would you?" she quietly asked.

Sage thumbed through her appointment book. "Well, as a matter of fact, I am free at 11:30 a.m. if that works for you? It's actually called Reiki."

"Oh, yes, then that would be perfect. She will probably be having lunch about that time," the woman whispered again as she wildly glanced around.

"Okay. Good," Sage whispered back. "Your name, please?"

"My name? Do you really need my name?"

"Ummm… yes, I do, and there is a short form I will need you to fill out ahead of time, as well."

"Oh, dear." The woman looked quite pale and rattled. "Will it stay just between us?"

"Oh, yes! Everything that goes on here is held in the strictest confidence, I assure you."

"Well, alright then. My name is Mrs. Vivian Wright."

Sage had to put her head down and glance off to the side to hide her smile. She knew she should have recognized this odd woman, even with the disguise. This was one of Mrs. Chamberlain's cohorts. Now this was making some sense and the *she* having lunch must be Mrs. Chamberlain. She shook off her grin, wrote Mrs. Wright's name down, and watched her slink out the door. As Sage observed her scurry down Main Street, she was quite disappointed she would be unable to share this little scenario with anyone.

It was two days since Keenan's "after-effects" and he was up early organizing their luggage into the vehicle while Tessy was saying good-bye to everyone. It had been a long while since he had visited Ashling Manor, and he was looking forward to seeing the grand old structure. The drive from Winnipeg to Ladyslipper, however, was a different story. Driving that many miles back in Ireland on the motorway, you could almost be from one end of the country to the other. The vastness of Canada always amazed him.

It wasn't long and they were passing open fields being worked and seeded with an army of gigantic farm machinery. Their size alone impressed the onlookers. They chatted about relatives in Ireland, all of Tessy's nieces and nephews she was so looking forward to spending time with very soon. They purposely tried very hard not to talk about the little packages that were soon to be revealed. But they were very much on their minds. They stopped for a bite in Brandon, then Keenan asked if he could drive the last leg of their journey. Reluctantly, Tessy gave in.

"Now, ye do remember which side of the road you're to be on?" she asked as she gingerly handed him the keys.

"The roads over here are so big, does it really matter?" Keenan answered with a dry smile.

"Aye, it does matter a great deal. And if ye don't behave I'll be asking ye to hand those keys back to me."

Keenan just laughed and jumped in to the driver's seat. "Get in and hang on!" he quipped.

Much to Tessy's dismay, the last part of the trip was a mite quicker than usual.

As they pulled into the lane of Ashling Manor, Keenan let out a sigh, "Aye, there she is, then. Lookin' as pretty and proud as ever."

"Aye, 'tis a sight for sore eyes, to be sure," Tessy readily agreed.

As Tessy opened the door the dogs trampled over them both. The last time Keenan had seen Duke and Darby they were just puppies, but they remembered him well. Keenan lay on the grass and let them lick and run all over him.

"Keenan O'Connor! Get up! You're teaching them all sorts of bad tricks. Duke, Darby, come here, good dogs," and she lavished them with pats and hugs. The cats, on the other hand, were nowhere to be seen and probably wouldn't be until their fragile egos were healed and they figured they had punished Tessy long enough.

Keenan headed up to his regular room with his luggage in hand. It was close to supper so Tessy went to the kitchen to pull a cottage pie out of the freezer. She had a couple of stout in the fridge, and when Keenan entered the room she handed him one.

"Don't mind if I do." Keenan took it and stepped over to the cupboard and pulled out two mugs.

They spent the next couple of hours enjoying their pints and the cottage pie. When they were done, they took their tea into the living room and spent some time looking through Auntie Shannon's old photo albums and reminiscing. Then, without a word, they simultaneously set their cups down on the coffee table and looked at one another. Tessy followed Keenan up the stairs, and they each went into their rooms to get the wee parcels. Tessy opened the drawer and there it was, exactly where she had put it all those months ago. She had not even ventured to touch it before this! When she returned to the living room, Keenan was waiting for her.

"Well, I guess this is it, then?" he said as he held up the box.

"Aye, 'tis time." Tessy slowly sat down beside her brother.

"Well, with ye being the oldest, I guess ye should go first." Keenan solemnly looked at his sister.

Tessy just scowled at him and picked up her box. It was neatly tied with a faded satin ribbon. She untethered the bleached tie and forced open the lid to find a cotton square covering the treasure. Both she and Keenan were leaning so far over the box their heads were touching. Tessy lifted the cotton and there was an amulet. She carefully removed it from its resting place, realizing the last person to have touched it would have been her mother. She brought it to her lips and kissed it for that very reason. Next, she noticed its weight and craftsmanship. It was unquestionably very old. On the front she recognized the Haggerty coat of arms, which made sense being as it came from their mother. She turned it over to reveal an inscription written in Gaelic.

She looked at Keenan, who had not yet spoken a word. "How's y'er Gaelic?" she asked with raised eyebrows.

"Ye know, darn well, that ye were always better at it than me."

"I was afraid ye were going to say that. I sure wish one of us had paid more attention when Mam was trying to teach it to us. Never mind. Open yours; maybe that will give us a clue."

He, too, ceremoniously opened his box to find a ring which matched the amulet, with the Haggerty coat of arms and the same Gaelic inscription on the inside.

"Well, that didn't help us out much. I never saw mother with either of these, did ye?" Tessy asked.

"Nye. Neither one."

They each examined them one more time before they returned them to their encasings. Tessy was having difficulty fixing the lid onto her box when she turned it over and noticed a note wedged up into it. She pulled it out and carefully opened the faded, tattered piece of paper. It, too, was written in Gaelic.

"It's odd that there was nothing said of this in the reading of the will," Tessy absently remarked as she turned the paper over, looking for more.

"Aye. But these really had nothing to do with Aunt Shannon other than she was the keeper. And she did deliver them as she promised she would."

"Aye. 'Tis true. But Aunt Shannon was a Haggerty, as well. Granted, Mam was the oldest and therefore, they were probably entrusted to her, but after she was gone you'd think they would have been passed on. I think, for now anyway, the less said about these to anyone the better. Just until we figure out a bit more."

"Aye. I think you're right," Keenan agreed.

They sat and finished their tea in silence and deep in thought.

32
Preparations and Bookings Begin

And so it was that even though the contents of the wee packages were revealed, the mystery remained. They hadn't mentioned them to anyone so their little secret was safe. Tessy was uncomfortable keeping this from Marshall, but she thought it best – at least, for now. She wanted to get the Gaelic translated first to see if it would all make sense. She recognized a few of the words but would definitely need some assistance with the majority of it. Besides, she also had a wedding, in just three short weeks, to get ready for. The mystery would have to wait.

Marshall, Dotty and Bert were arriving a week prior to the wedding, and she had plenty to do before then. Keenan tried his best to help but, truth be known, he really just got in the way. Finally, Tessy suggested, to keep him busy, he go over to the Bakers and see if there was something that Danny and Tommy needed his help with. That turned out much better for all!

The tent, tables, chairs, popcorn machine and the portable toilets had all been ordered and would be delivered two days preceding the big day. But there was much more to be done. Tessy was making homemade granola as wedding favours and packaging it in windowed brown paper bags with decorative stickers displaying their names, date of the wedding, and the ingredients. She would make two different kinds: one with fruits and nuts, and one without the nuts for anyone with allergies. She prepared and packaged the ones without nuts first. She was on the second batch when the hardware store called to let her know the small mason jars she had ordered were in. She was using them as votives for the tables, with a little white sand, a couple of small sea shells, and a tea light set inside, and with some tulle tied around the outside rim. She thought them to be simple, inexpensive, yet functional and pretty. That was basically the theme Tessy and Marshall had decided on… mainly because that was the way Tessy lived. Marshall, on the other hand, would have spent a fortune just to be married to such a lady.

Tessy did send Keenan out to the back forest one day to collect dead broken branches. She was planning on fastening them to the tent poles, then stringing mini lights and tulling, with a few white feathers attached to them. She was also going to need some twisted willow branches to make a large, rustic chandelier with mini lights to hang from the center of the tent. She wanted the setting to feel attractive, and to ensure that Mother Nature was invited and very welcomed. She now had all four elements included, branches for Earth, feathers for Air, candles for Fire, white sand and shells for Water. Aye, it was subtle yet very significant.

The kids were over almost every day to see what they could help with. This event had them beside themselves with excitement, that, and the fact that they were enjoying their newest uncle very much. Uncle Keenan constantly teased them and made them laugh. Tessy would watch, shake her head, and laugh along. How she wished she and Keenan lived closer… maybe someday.

Tessy had just arrived home from her visit at the seniors' center, where she volunteered every Tuesday morning, when the phone rang. She scooted down the hall to pick up on the second ring.

"Good mornin'," she huffed.

"Good morning, my sweet bride-to-be."

Tessy could hear the smile Marshall held on his handsome face.

"Oh, love, how are ye today?"

"Better now that I have heard your voice."

Tessy laughed.

"Were you down at the center this morning?"

"Aye. Just walked in the door."

"Good. I have some wonderful news. Brian, Anna and the kids flew in from Switzerland last night and are here with us."

"Oh, Marshall! How grand! Ye must be in seventh heaven. First having Kyle home and now Brian."

"Yeah… man… it's great to see them. Luca and Alina have grown a foot since I saw them last."

"Aye. They grow like weeds at that age. How wonderful for ye. Can't wait to put my arms around them."

"Honey, that's kind of why I'm calling. I don't think there's going to be room at Penny's for everyone, and Brian and Anna were thinking it would be better for them to be off on their own a bit. Do you know of some place they could rent for their time in Ladyslipper?"

"Let me think, dear." Tessy hummed for a minute. "Aye. I think I might have an idea. Let me make a phone call and I'll ring ye right back."

"Thanks, sweetheart. I was pretty sure you'd come up with something."

They hung up and Tessy was on it. She pulled the phone book out of the drawer and thumbed through the pages until she found the number she was looking for. Twenty minutes later she was dialing Marshall back.

"Hi, love. Well, I called Stewart out at the lake. He has a few cabins there that they rent for the summer. They are not open yet and are in the process of getting them cleaned right at the moment, but he says they could have one ready for us by the wedding. Do ye think they'd be wantin' something like that?"

"That sounds great! Just let me check with them. Hang on."

Tessy could hear the children screeching with excitement in the background.

"You probably got that as a big, fat, Yes! Thank you so much, sweetheart."

"Aye," Tessy chuckled. "You're very welcome, love. I'll give them a ring and book it, then. I'm sure they'll have a grand time there, and it's still nice and close to all the weddin' fun."

"How are you doing with all the preparations?"

"Oh, they are coming along just as fine as frog's fur."

"Well, that's good, but I sure wish you would have let me come out and help you like I wanted."

"There's not much for ye to do, yet, but don't ye be fearin'… I'll keep ye busier than a one-armed bandit when ye get here."

Marshall laughed. "I bet you will."

33
Organized and Penalized

Things were happening now! Marshall, Dotty and Bert arrived, and Tessy had lists for everyone. Exactly one week before the big day, they were all in the kitchen discussing their appointed duties when the kids came thundering in the back door. Tessy soon had tasks for them, too. She sent the boys off, including Marshall and Bert, to construct both a popcorn stand and a lemonade stand. She had already somewhat designed them, so there wouldn't be too much meeting of the minds. Emma and Becky were directed out to the picnic table to put one scoop of sand into each mason jar, while Sarah and Cherokee would strategically place the shells and tea lights in them, then tie the tulle around them. Keenan had just left for the airport to pick up his Mary. This meant everyone was gone, and Dotty and Tessy were finally left in peace and quiet.

"Wow! You're good. Where on earth did you learn to do that?" Dotty smiled with her hands on her hips and shaking her head.

"Being a teacher for twenty-five years ye learn a thing or two about delegating," she laughed. "Now, we can get baking."

Dotty was honoured when Tessy asked her to do the wedding cake, so the less going on in the kitchen the better. They had no time for any mishaps or do-overs!

And so, as the week wore on that is how it went, everyone pitching in, with Tessy keeping everything organized and running like a fine tuned engine. Family and guests were arriving at different intervals throughout the week and being billeted here and there. Brian, Anna, Luca and Alina made it out early to do some holidaying and to help out where they could. Sarah was staying at Cherokee's for the week and Matt was at Brendon's, so that way Penny and Jim could accommodate Janie when she arrived tomorrow, and Kellie "if and when" she arrived. Marshall would be spending the two nights prior to the wedding there as well, just on tradition and principle. Tessy insisted! To everyone's surprise, there was word that Grandma Tucker was attending and she was bringing a guest and had made arrangements at a nearby bed and breakfast. Tessy also heard from Sage that her Mom and younger sister were going to make the wedding after all. Tessy was delighted, and invited them to come stay with her. She still had one room left after billeting Dotty, Bert, Keenan and Mary. It was decided that Rosemary would stay with Tessy, and Saffron would cozy up with Sage. Aye, it was all coming together, and how fun to have Ashling Manor bursting with loving family and friends. Tessy was hoping Dermot was close by to enjoy all the excitement. She hadn't had much time to spend with him lately, but she would definitely find a moment to have a chat before Saturday.

Before they knew it, the tent had arrived and was being erected. The men, of course, were all outside trying to give the delivery people a hand, but they were mainly getting in the way. Soon it was up and ready for decorating. Tessy showed everyone the design and delegated the next set of steps. The guys set up the tables and chairs, and the ladies began working their magic. Tessy had ordered bolts of muslin to cover the tables as well as the backs of the chairs, along with wide satin ribbon to tie around them. When it was done it looked enchanting.

The next morning the women spent out in Tessy's cutting garden, picking hundreds of daisy blossoms to place in the mis-matched fine china bowls Tessy had purchased at the second hand shops. They would accompany the mason jars as centerpieces on the tables. Tessy and Rosemary would tend to that the next morning while Dotty and Mary saw to things in the kitchen. The day had flown by with last-minute preparations. The men had gone to the liquor store to get the license and the booze, then came back to set up the bar. Matt, Brendon and Jason were setting up the DJ booth, as they were taking care of the music for the evening, for which Tessy and Marshall had made most of the selections. Tommy had come over to cut the grass, whipper-snip, and get the yard looking pristine. The girls primped and fluffed all the tulle and feathers to perfection, and the ladies had the kitchen smelling like heaven. Dotty was smoothing the last bit of cream icing on the wedding cake. It was three tiers of carrot cake topped with orange buttercream icing made with Grand Marnier. Tomorrow it would be delicately decorated with viola and alyssum blossoms from the garden, then placed on a circular platter approximately three inches larger than the bottom tier, made of small fresh willow twigs nailed together. The final result would be stunning.

Tessy and Marshall were having a commissioner from the area to officiate the ceremony, and since they had met with her on a number of occasions over the past few months, they weren't sure whether they needed to bother her for the rehearsal. However, she said she was available and didn't mind popping by, and that it would probably just make things a little easier for tomorrow.

They were just about to get started when they heard a horn beep and a car door slam shut.

"Where the hell is everyone?" a female voice called out.

Marshall looked at Tessy, scowled, and shook his head. "That, I believe, would be my youngest daughter," he sighed. "Excuse me. I apologize, everyone, I will be right back." Penny, Brian, Janie and Kyle followed him.

After the embarrassing start they continued and everything went off without a hitch.

Penny and Jim insisted on having the rehearsal dinner at their place, with family and friends invited for a barbeque. Soon after the rehearsal, the Tuckers' backyard was filled with people enjoying a lovely, relaxing evening. Toasts were made to the happy couple with laughter and good wishes filling the air. Keenan kept everyone amused with his Irish quotes and blessings. He did, however, behave himself with his Mary keeping a close watch.

Sage and Tommy were cuddled by the fire with Saffron not far from them. They were getting to know Janie, Kyle and Kellie better. Sage skipped off to check with her Mom about something, and that was when Kellie slipped in close beside Tommy.

"Hi," she whispered as she ran her long, manicured, florescent orange fingernail along Tommy's forearm.

"Ummm... hi," Tommy answered as he blushed and moved back from her.

"Oh, don't go away. I just thought we should get to know one another better. Do ya' wanna skip this drag and go for a ride?"

"Ummm… no, thank you," he said as he wildly glanced around hoping for someone to rescue him. He didn't want to be rude to Marshall's daughter, but he had never dealt with anyone quite so blunt. Everyone was engrossed in conversation and hadn't noticed their interaction.

Tessy spotted them from across the yard and was pretty sure what was taking place. She was on her way over to save him when she caught a glimpse of Sage out of the corner of her eye, marching towards Tommy with fire in her Irish eyes.

"Oh my, this could get nasty," Tessy flinched, watching with great interest!

Sage stood tall over Kellie. "Excuse me!" she glared. "You are in my spot."

"I didn't see your name on it," Kellie smirked at her.

"Trust me, my name is all over it! Right, Tommy?"

"You bet, babe," Tommy grinned with pride. "Kellie, I suggest you find someone else to harass. That's my girl, and you do not want to see her angry."

By this time, Penny had clued in to what was going on. "Kellie! I need to have a word with you in the house. NOW!"

As Tessy witnessed Penny escort Kellie into the house, she was thinking she would, somehow, find time to concoct a special tea and send it over to the Tuckers' in the morning.

It was getting on in the evening, so before everyone starting departing, Brian clinked his beer bottle with a metal knife as his family, siblings, and Dotty and Bert came up on the deck and stood by him.

"I have something I'd like to say to the bride and groom. Well, really more of something to present to the bride and groom. Dad, Tessy, if you would please join us up here for a moment?"

Marshall took Tessy's hand and they ascended the steps.

"Now, we know this is a little early but we wanted to present this gift certificate tonight to show you how happy we are for you and to welcome Tessy to our crew… as motley as it may be!"

Everyone chuckled, then remained silent as they watched Marshall open the envelope. His eyes grew wide and he handed it to Tessy. She gasped and flung around to gaze at her new family. The guests were calling out, "What is it?" Tessy handed it back to Marshall and he held it up. "It's a gift certificate for three nights' accommodation at a castle in Ireland!" He and Tessy began hugging their family members. There was an uproar of wows, claps and cheers.

It was just before midnight when Marshall walked Tessy up to her door. He lovingly gazed into her beautiful green eyes and sighed.

"I can't believe tomorrow is almost here. I am the happiest man on earth."

Tessy smiled and quipped, "Aye. Your last night of freedom."

Marshall came back with, "No! My last night of loneliness, without you."

He gently gathered her in his arms and kissed her goodnight, for the final time in his life as a single man.

34
Promises of Forever After

Tessy was up at the crack of dawn. She quietly crept downstairs to let the dogs out and get some coffee brewing for her guests. She got it underway, then slipped down the hall to the library to spend some quality time with Dermot. She softly closed the door behind her, slowly eased herself into the large mahogany chair at the big desk, and lovingly stroked it.

"Well, Dermot, my love, this is it. What ye had planned has finally come about. I know you're here with me now, and ye eternally will be, and for that, I thank ye. I've constantly counted on your subtle guidance and strength, and you've never let me down, and for that, too, I thank ye. Oh Dermot, as much as I love Marshall, I do miss ye. As I said before, I don't want ye going anywhere. I'll need ye for times when no one else understands. Ye are my rock and now my guardian angel, and for that, I thank ye! I'm sure ye already know, that out of love and respect, I'm keeping your name." She heard someone rustling in the kitchen. "God love ye, Dermot McGuigan." When she turned to walk out, she felt a peck on the cheek and incredible warmth fill her heart. She smiled and brushed a tear away as she gently closed the door and stepped into her new life.

Tessy took a minute to take in a deep breath before heading into the kitchen. It was Dotty bustling around preparing for breakfast like she had been raised in that kitchen. That woman does live to fuss, Tessy mused.

"Mornin' Dotty," Tessy smiled.

Dotty swung around. "Oh, good morning, Tess. How did you sleep?"

"Better than expected, for sure; however, I did place some lavender, hops and chamomile in a pouch and stuck it between my pillows."

"Good. I'm glad to hear it. It's going to be a long, exciting day." Dotty reached over and hugged Tess. "I'm so happy for you and the good doctor," she whimpered as she flicked tears off her cheeks.

"Now, don't be startin' any of that, already!" Tessy playfully scolded.

"Oh, I know. I'm just going to be like a faucet this afternoon."

Tessy chuckled, gently patting and rubbing her friend on the back.

Dotty collected herself and poured them each a cup of coffee. Tessy took hers and went to sit at the table when she remembered she wanted to make up that tea mix to send over to the Tuckers.

"Dotty, dear, would ye mind standing guard for me, for a few minutes, while I step into the back kitchen to make up a little something special? I'd care not to be disturbed and with a house full of people I'm not sure that would be possible," she chuckled.

"I'd be happy to," Dotty knowingly smiled.

Tessy slipped into the mysterious little room and began pulling mason jars and sacks down from the shelves and setting them on her working table. Into a tin she dumped a little of this and poured a little of that and while she did so, she chanted:

This tea I blend is to keep trouble at bay.
To make things run smoothly, come what may.
Though you think you are clever and need to be heard,
Sometimes silence is the most powerful word.
No matter the day, be gloomy or bright
Make those who sample this, act proper and right.
I ask the Divine to hear and grant my plea
As this is my will — so mote it be.

Tessy finished just in time as it wasn't long and the kitchen was a hub of activity. Some were having coffee for now, some were eating, while others were pulling out platters and such for the day's big event. Keenan was very relieved to have Bert there as backup. He couldn't imagine being the only guy in a house full of wedding-ecstatic women. After breakfast, Tessy sent the men over to the Tuckers' with the tin. She had already called Penny with instructions.

Even though Marshall wasn't allowed over to Ashling Manor until closer to the big moment, there were still things to be done and he did have a list of duties: to confirm their hotel reservations for tonight, and to pick up his tux from the drycleaners, and the other tuxes from the rental shop.

Tessy and Marshall wanted to include all the children and make sure no one felt left out. The original wedding party had consisted of Cherokee and Sarah standing up with Tessy and Brian and Kyle standing up with Marshall, with Emma and Becky as flower girls. However, when Sage entered Tessy's life, she asked Marshall if he minded enlarging the group by one each. Marshall, of course, had no objections and asked Bert if he would help usher. Bert, being the "don't put me in any spotlights kinda guy," said he was honoured, but if he could find someone else that would be better. Marshall just laughed and asked Jim. Matt was to assist Kyle and Jim with the usher duties, while Luca and Alina were to organize the children's activity table. Yes, they all felt significant and appreciated with their assigned roles.

Things were moving along and running like clockwork. Sarah and Cherokee begged Tessy to let them come over early and do her hair and makeup just like they did the night of Tessy and Marshall's first date. Tessy laughed at that memory and eagerly agreed; it was, after all, almost a prerequisite, as they were her bridesmaids.

Before the girls arrived, Tessy went out into her cutting garden to pick her wedding bouquet. She had no real plan ahead of time; she knew the flowers would come from her garden, but she wouldn't know what was at its peak until that morning. She spotted her pale pink peonies coming into bloom. They were magnificent. She snipped a couple just open enough that they would be perfect. She included some daisies to coordinate with the ones on the guest tables, and then she added some pink yarrow. It had come early this year, and the feathery, fern-like greenery with the lovely flat pink tops would give the bouquet a light airy touch. She played with the flowers, arranging them this way and that, and when she was pleased with the selection, she placed them in the pail and headed back to the house. She stopped and looked up at the grand structure. "Oh, Ashling Manor! What stories of love and laughter you must have. Thank you for my time with you. You know my happiness, my pain, and my sorrow. Thank you for welcoming all the loving family and dear friends that have crossed over your threshold and entered into my heart. I thank you for keeping me warm and protected. I know, as well, that you have your secrets." She hesitated, then added, "And, unfortunately, so do I." Tessy suddenly felt a pang of guilt. How could she think of getting married and still hold a secret from this incredible man? What on earth was she afraid of? That was it! She would share this Haggerty mystery with the man she loved and was about to marry. And she would find Keenan immediately, and suggest he do the same with his Mary.

When Tessy got back to the house, Sage and Saffron were already there. Penny drove the girls over, soon after, and helped them carry in their dresses, which they had each chosen themselves, their shoes, backpacks and other wedding paraphernalia. The level of energy and excitement at Ashling Manor was unimaginable. Penny stayed for a while, but had to return home and get Emma bathed and dressed. Keenan and Bert were out on the back deck with the dogs, staying out of the way, and having a beer. They wanted nothing to do with the female frenzy that was going on inside!

Sarah and Cherokee performed their magic on Tessy, just as before. She looked radiant! She remained in her housecoat while she helped the girls get ready. No one had seen her dress yet, and she decided to keep it a surprise. The girls were disappointed, but understood. They did, however, help her with her simple headdress when they styled her hair. She had made it herself. It was a band of tiny cream-coloured satin flowers that fit around her head with a small spray of tulle gathered at the back that lay just above her shoulders. It looked lovely.

When Sage told Tessy that her Mom and Saffron were coming to the wedding, she also informed Tessy that Saffron was a budding photographer and would be more than happy to take some pictures, if she wanted. Tessy and Marshall jumped at the suggestion. So as everyone was getting ready she took some candid shots that were relaxed and fun. She also popped over to the Tuckers' to take some shots of the groom and groomsmen, as well.

Everyone was ready, the guys had just arrived, and the yard was filling up with anxious guests. Tessy had shooed the girls off and was standing at her bedroom window looking through the lace curtains at the animation below. Her mind was reeling with thoughts and emotions. How did this happen? How, in just one short year, did her whole world change? *Oh, Dermot, I wish ye were here to hold me and tell me everything will be okay.* She was ready to cry but then she remembered her makeup and scolded herself. She heard something and turned to see the picture she kept of Dermot on her dresser had tipped over. She walked over to it and picked it up. The strong scent of Old Spice, Dermot's favourite aftershave, was hanging heavy in the air, and she knew. She knew he was there with her and that he was letting her know that it is time for her to move on.

"Alright, love. I hear ye loud and clear. God love ye… I know I do."

She put the picture back up where it belonged and opened her closet door. Hanging on the inside of the door was the dress. She had ordered it from one of her favourite specialty shops in Ireland. It was what they called a medieval Guinevere design, a long, slim gown, cream, featuring a sweetheart neckline with shimmering ivory cording crossed over and around the bodice, then hanging to the gown's hemline at the front, with long sheer bell sleeves to complete it. She slipped it on and stood in front of her large oval mahogany mirror while she tied the cord loosely around her body. She looked like a goddess that had just stepped out of a book of Druids.

Dermot's picture fell over again, hard!

Tessy laughed out loud. "Well, thank ye, love."

She was adjusting and straightening the cord when she heard a ruckus going on downstairs, so she took one more look in the mirror then ran out to see what was going on.

It seemed to be coming from the kitchen. She hurried down the hall and into the mayhem. There stood, of all people, Mrs. Chamberlain!

"What, in St. Paddy's name, is going on?" Tessy yelled over the commotion.

Everyone stopped and stared at the goddess.

Tessy broke the silence. "Mrs. Chamberlain, is there something I can help ye with? If ye haven't noticed, we're kinda' in the middle of something." She felt a little bad being so abrupt but, after all, this was her wedding day.

"Yes! Your so-called partner in crime has been working her witchcraft on my friend, Mrs. Wright, and I want her to stop. NOW! God only knows how much damage she's already done!"

"Mrs. Chamberlain, first, this is not the time nor place to discuss this, and second, it really isn't any of your business what Sage does, or Mrs. Wright, for that matter."

"We'll see about that! Now, I'll let you get back to your witch's ceremony. Good day!" Mrs. Chamberlain stomped out and slammed the screen door.

"Well, I think we'll be needin' to burn a little sage and lavender to clear this negative energy in here before we proceed any further," Tessy huffed as she headed for the herbal kitchen.

It took a while, but everyone settled down and the mood soon returned to the furor of the joyous occasion. The girls followed Tessy back up to her room, clamouring about how gorgeous she looked, and how well she handled the situation, and how beautiful the ceremony is going to be. Tessy just laughed and shook her head at their overzealousness. She still had her jewelry to put on and her shoes, then she'd be ready. And, good thing, as this little episode had set them back a few minutes.

Marshall, totally oblivious to what had just taken place, was starting to get a little concerned. As he paced, he was hoping it wasn't because Tessy had changed her mind. To find out why they were running behind schedule, he finally sent Brian to the house. He came back chuckling.

Marshall looked puzzled. "What?"

"I guess some old biddy came by the house screaming and yelling about witches or something."

Marshall immediately knew who it was but couldn't for the life of him figure out why, especially today of all days. "Well, that certainly explains the delay."

One wedding extravagance they did agree upon was the harpist. She was softly playing beautiful Celtic tunes while everyone patiently waited. All of a sudden she stopped and began playing the tune they had picked for Tessy's entrance. Marshall's heart stopped and he took a deep breath. This is it!

Everyone rose and turned to watch the procession. Emma and Becky were so adorable. They each had a basket of rose petals that they gently scattered down the aisle way. People were ahhhing and taking pictures. Next came Sage. She was a knockout! Tommy couldn't believe how lucky he was to be dating this beauty. His smile couldn't help but tell the whole world. Sarah was next and, wow, Penny couldn't help but tear up at how grown she looked. She was such a beautiful young lady. Cherokee followed, looking just as beautiful and all grown up. Her mother, Skye, and father, Cache, were so proud of her. Then from around the corner the goddess appeared. You could almost hear the gasps of awe. Much to everyone's surprise, Bert was walking her down the aisle. Yes, the "keep me out of the limelight kinda' guy," couldn't say no to Tessy. They had, actually, arranged it months ago, but he was sworn to secrecy and that was the real reason he had to turn down Marshall. This was one secret, however, Tessy didn't mind keeping from Marshall.

When Marshall caught a glimpse of his bride he immediately filled with emotion and tears sprang to his eyes. She was breathtaking. He couldn't take his eyes off this stunning Celtic goddess walking towards him. He'd seen her glow many times in the past, but today, at this moment, she was luminous. In those minutes that it took for her to reach him, time stood still. Just as she got to his side a tear dropped on to his cheek. Tessy smiled, reached up and gently wiped it from her beloved.

Marshall, too, smiled, took her hand in his and kissed it.

The commissioner began, "Good afternoon and welcome." She smiled out over the wedding party and guests. "We are here at this joyous occasion to support and witness Marshall Allan Tayse and Tessy Margaret McGuigan join together in matrimony. As they already know, it is not to be entered into thoughtlessly. It is a lifetime commitment that promises love, respect, honour and devotion. They have agreed to support and comfort each other in times of joy as well as sorrow. They will laugh together, grieve together, and grow together in love. With this understanding, Marshall and Tessy wish to be joined in marriage. Therefore, if any person can show just reason why these two persons may not be joined in matrimony, let them now declare reasons, or else from this time forward, keep their peace."

Penny threw Kellie a wicked glare and held it, making sure she understood the severity of it. Thankfully, there was a moment of silence. Penny smiled to herself. Once again Tessy's tea had, obviously, done the trick.

The commissioner continued, "Marshall and Tessy have written their own vows and would now like to share them with you. Marshall, you may start."

Marshall held Tessy's free hand and looked lovingly into her Irish eyes. "Tessy, I knew the minute I was first in your presence and touched your hand, that my life would be forever changed. You are the most beautiful, magical woman I have ever met, both inside and out. I promise to support you, respect you, and honour you, but most of all, love you with all my heart. I've said it before and I'll say it again, I am the luckiest man on earth and I will be devoted to you until, and beyond, I have taken my last breath."

Tessy's eyes were flooded and about to overflow.

The commissioner kindly smiled, waited a moment for Tessy to gather herself, then said, "Tessy. Your vows."

"Marshall, my love. It may have taken me a mite longer to realize I was so in love with ye, but I am, and I couldn't be more blessed than if the good Lord himself walked in to this room. Ye are a kind, generous man. Ye are a man of your word, one to be trusted to the very end. Though there are times when ye can be a bit of a scallywag, truth be told." She waited for the laughter to cease. "Ye are a healer of the people and now the healer of my heart. I, too, promise to respect, honour and support you in any way I can, and will be devoted to the end. I'm going to finish with an ancient Celtic wedding vow that sums up who I am and how I feel." She took a breath, and chanted:

Ye are blood of my blood, and bone of my bone.

I give ye my body, that we two might be one.
I give ye my spirit, 'til our life shall be done.
You cannot possess me for I belong to myself.
But while we both wish it, I give you that which is mine to give.
You cannot command me, for I am a free person.
But I shall serve you in those ways you require.
And the honeycomb will taste sweeter coming from my hand.

The commissioner smiled again. "Having declared these marriage vows, we will now exchange the rings. Marshall, repeat after me... Tessy, I give you this ring as a symbol of my love and commitment to you." Marshall repeated the statement and slipped a ring on Tessy's finger. Tessy repeated the words and placed a ring on Marshall's finger.

"Now, by the authority vested in me by the Province of Saskatchewan, I pronounce you husband and wife. Marshall, you may kiss your bride." The yard immediately erupted with cheers and clapping.

The day was filled with laughter, fine food, drink and enchantment. There were toasts to be made, pictures to be taken, and friends and family to share memorable moments with. They danced into the late evening, and before they knew it, it was time for them to leave and start their life, truly as one. Tessy and Marshall changed out of their wedding clothes and stood outside Ashling Manor saying goodbye. Tessy called all the single girls to get lined up. She was ready to toss the bouquet. She stood on the top step, turned around, then peeked back to make sure everyone was ready and tossed it high into the air. As it sailed up, up, up, then tumbled on its way down, the girls were screaming and reaching, but when it did finally stop, it was in Sage's clutches. They all laughed and cheered for her. Tessy ran down the steps and gave her a big hug. "A good sign, to be sure," she told her with a wink.

Marshall held the car door for his bride, made sure she was settled in, and closed it. He ran around, jumped into the driver's seat, beeped the horn, and they were off. He looked over at Tessy, picked up her hand, and kissed it. "Well, my love. Let's go start a life of love and laughter."

Tessy just laughed. "Aye. That we shall."

35
Adieu to a Spirit and Embracing the Hereafter

Tessy and Marshall were exhausted when they reached the hotel. It had been a long couple of days and they were both feeling the effects. Therefore, it wasn't the night of passion some would expect, but instead a night to be as one, talking, cuddling, and enjoying glasses of champagne. Tessy shared the Haggerty mystery with her husband, and they had fun concocting all sorts of yarns around this enigma. They decided it would accompany them to Ireland, as they were sure the key to unraveling this mystery would be found in the homeland. The passion they lacked that evening was made up for the next morning before they left.

As they were driving into Ladyslipper, they spotted the party rental delivery truck pulling out of Tessy's driveway.

"Well, I guess that means the tent is down," Marshall concluded.

"Aye. Rather sad. Weeks of preparations, then over in an instant."

When they pulled up to Ashling Manor, everyone was outside and came over to greet the newlyweds. After they got caught up, they all headed into the house. As soon as Tessy stepped in to Ashling Manor, she sensed something was different. Even though she was in the presence of the man she loved and dear family and friends, she felt a strange loneliness. She needed to go to the library, but was unable to discreetly do so right at the moment. She would find a quiet time a little later.

Keenan and Mary were leaving for Ireland the next day, so Tessy wanted to have a special evening for them. She and Dotty insisted on making Dotty's famous prime rib roast with Yorkshire pudding and all the trimmings. It would be served in the dining room. Dotty, just being Dotty, already had most everything prepared before Tessy got home. Tessy knew she would be seeing her brother and sister-in-law very soon, but she always felt sad when Keenan left, as she never knew if or when he'd ever be back to Ashling Manor. They had a wonderful evening of amusing stories and laughter. Marshall got privy to more tales of Tessy's younger years. While Tessy scolded Keenan, she did return the odd yarn of some of Keenan's outlandish antics, including a few which he wished had been left in the cubby.

Everyone was ready to retire, and Tessy thought this a good time to go to the library. She went to her bedroom first to take the picture of Dermot off her dresser, out of respect for Marshall. She would take it to the library and place it on the bookshelf with the other pictures she kept there. She opened the library door, went over to the desk lamp, switched it on, then closed the door. The room was empty; Dermot wasn't there. She felt a pang in her heart. She stroked the top of the desk, as she always did, when she needed Dermot to appear. Nothing. Tears flooded her eyes. She let them drop off her cheeks and on to the desk. No, no, this cannot happen. Dermot, I told you, I will always need you close by. Where are you? She waited for a time for an answer. Nothing. She dried her eyes, switched off the light and made her way to the door. Just as she grasped the door handle his picture fell over. She smiled, closed her eyes, and said a prayer of gratitude.

As she made her way up to bed, she knew that Dermot was just letting her know that it was time for him to back away and let Marshall be the main male figure in her life. As usual, this was another time he was right. She would stop relying on Dermot for all the answers. She was starting a brand new life with an amazing, kind and generous man who loved her very much. And she truly did love him. "I hear ye, Dermot McGuigan. I will let go," she whispered as she reached the top landing.

Marshall and Tessy would be driving Keenan and Mary to the airport in Regina. They were making a connecting flight to Toronto, then on to Dublin. It was going to be a very long twenty-four hours before they were actually home. Their flight left at 12:30 p.m., so they were up and going early.

The kids all made it over to say good-bye to their favourite new uncle and aunt. They begged Keenan to get computer savvy so they could stay in touch. Mary promised she'd make him work hard at it. Sarah and Cherokee, now that Sarah had relatives in Ireland, promised they would be over for a visit as soon as they graduated. As they drove down the lane, Keenan was hanging out the back window yelling all sorts of Irish blessings over the children. When Mary finally pulled him back in, he had to wipe some tears.

"God love every one of those little tykes," he choked.

"Aye. Ye know He does, love," Mary sympathized with her emotional husband.

On the way they discussed the amulet and ring. They would set aside some time while they were all together in Ireland to do some investigating. Now that the two couples knew about mystery, it was quite exhilarating to think what they might find. Maybe nothing… but what if? Tessy was getting more and more excited about her trip all the time. Then Keenan asked a question that changed the excitement to apprehension.

"So what day have ye set up for the handfasting?"

"The what!" Marshall blurted.

Tessy was planning on breaking this news to Marshall sometime this week before they left; however, today was not going to be that day, up until now.

"Keenan, sometimes I swear, ye open your big mouth before ye clear the rocks out of your brain!" Mary scolded.

"What?" he innocently shrugged.

"Marshall, I was going to tell ye all about it, but we've been so busy with the wedding that it just slipped my mind."

"Yes. The wedding. That means we're already married. Why would we need a handfasting?"

"Oh, so you do know what it's all about, then," Tessy flinched.

"Yes. It just so happens, that since I've fallen in love with an Irish lass, I have been doing a little research of my own."

"Bless your soul, love. How sweet."

"Don't try and butter me up. What's going on?"

Keenan piped up, "I'll tell ye what's going on. The women are going on and on and on. Tessy's cousins insist on a handfasting, come rain or shine. To them it's not a proper marriage until there's been a handfasting. And there'll be no hedging it, or ye won't get a moment's peace from that cackling group of hens."

"Keenan! Hush up and stop your carryin' on. 'Tis not your affair," Mary barked.

"Well, I'm just trying to save the poor lad."

"Thanks, Keenan. Nice to see someone has my back," Marshall smirked, then threw Tessy a look.

"Love, it's not as bad as Mr. Personality, back there, is making it out to be. I'll tell ye all about it before we get there, and we can even check some websites that will give a fair look."

"Well, if it's something that your relatives insist on and it's part of your heritage, I guess it won't do any harm to, at least, check it out."

"Thank ye, love. I appreciate that."

Keenan was about to give his two cents worth when Mary looked at him and warned, "Keenan O'Connor, if ye dare open your mouth, you'll be havin' a long, silent trip back to Ireland!"

They got to Regina in plenty of time to grab a bite before they dropped Keenan and Mary off at the airport. Tessy could hardly believe that Keenan was leaving already. The month seemed to have just flown by. She was looking forward to seeing him again, soon, in Ireland. They finished up and headed for the terminal.

There were hugs, handshakes and tender tears. Tessy and Marshall stood and watched them as they made their way to the departure gate. Finally, they turned, waved goodbye and disappeared.

Tessy looked up at Marshall with tears in her eyes. "As much of a pain in the arse that he is, I'm still gonna' miss him."

Marshall laughed, put his arm around his new bride, and they walked back out to the car.

The next couple of days were going to fly by. Tessy needed to make sure The Wee Nook of Herbals and Oils was heavily stocked to last the month and, of course, there was packing, final arrangements and last minute visiting with family. Brian, Anna and the kids were off tomorrow to holiday for the next month, heading out to BC, then back to Winnipeg. Kellie was already gone. Kyle was leaving for Winnipeg tomorrow, and Janie was staying with Penny for another week. Rosemary and Saffron would also be here another week. Dotty and Bert were really enjoying Ladyslipper, with all the kids and the animals, so it was decided that they would stay and look after Ashling Manor while Tessy and Marshall were gone, as Kyle would be back at the house in Winnipeg. Tessy was so thankful at how everything was falling into place so effortlessly. She was down at the pharmacy going over some orders with Jim when Eileen Tucker came in with her newest beau, Doug.

"Well, hello, you two," Jim smiled at his mother and shook Doug's hand.

Tessy gave Eileen a hug hello.

"What are you up to today, Mother?" Jim continued.

"Well, we just came by to see if Tessy and Marshall would like to meet us for dinner tonight. We would love to have a visit before we leave."

"Well, Eileen, that sounds lovely. Thank ye. I'll give Marshall a quick ring and make sure he's got nothing planned. I'll be back in a jiffy."

So it was arranged they would meet at the Inner Peace Bistro around 7 p.m.

Soon they were all seated and looking out over Ladyslipper Lake. This was a very special spot for Tessy and Marshall as it was the restaurant where they had enjoyed their first date getting to know one another. Eileen insisted they share the story of that night and poor Marshall's unfortunate mishap. They all had a good chuckle. The evening brought back wonderful memories of that blossoming romance.

Eileen and Doug were gone the next day. Tessy and Marshall would be flying out the day after tomorrow. Tessy's level of excitement was at its peak. She was in the extra spare bedroom going through their suitcases one more time when Marshall came in. He stood leaning up against the doorjamb with his arms crossed, smiling at his wife. "Hard to believe we're off to Ireland in another day. It just seems like yesterday when you were trying to figure out my riddles leading up to your gift opening of the tickets."

"Oh, don't remind me! What a scallywag ye were to be keeping me in the dark for as long as ye did."

Marshall laughed, walked over to his bride and kissed her. "Anything I can help you with?"

"Nye. Go on with ye," Tessy smiled back and slapped him on the butt.

The big day arrived and they were standing outside Ashling Manor with a large group of family and friends saying goodbye and wishing them a wonderful, safe holiday. Tessy turned to view Ashling Manor one more time and blew a kiss to her constant haven. After plenty of hugs and a few tears, they were pulling down the lane. Tessy looked at Marshall with such love and adoration.

"Thank you for this amazing trip. I don't think ye have any idea of what a gift it is. To be going back to my roots, seeing relatives I haven't seen for so long and, of course, for letting me have more time with my brother. You are a blessing, for sure, Marshall Allan Tayse."

Marshall picked up Tessy's hand and kissed it. "I am looking forward to sharing this adventure with you and seeing my Irish lass shine in her homeland. I have no idea what's in store, but I do know, as long as you're beside me, it's going to be fun."

They breezed through security, made their way on to the plane, and found their seats. This was it. They were on their first leg of the journey to Ireland. They would have a stop-over in Toronto and then be on their way. Tessy popped chewing gum in her mouth and offered one to Marshall. They heard the engines fire up, the flight attendant gave them their instructions, and they were soon taxiing down the runway. They stopped to wait their turn at the end. All of a sudden the engines roared, they picked up speed, faster, faster, faster... Tessy grabbed Marshall's arm and squeezed. Flying was not one of Tessy's favourite forms of transportation but rather necessary under the circumstances. She closed her eyes, chewed hard, and said a protection prayer. Marshall chuckled and just held her hand. Faster, faster, faster, lift off. Tessy's stomach was doing flip-flops. She opened one eye to see blue sky out the window. With Marshall's long, lanky legs he needed the aisle seat which meant she occupied the one in the middle. She was so glad she wouldn't have to see the ground below.

Marshall had no idea that Tessy was such a nervous flyer. "It's okay, honey, thousands of people do this every day."

"Well, I figure, if the good Lord wanted us to fly he woulda' put wings on our back."

Marshall laughed and kissed her hand.

An hour later, Tessy looked over at Marshall to find him sleeping. She pulled out the beautiful leather journal and pen he had given her just before Christmas. It had been tucked away for just this occasion. She began to write:

I begin these writings as we, Marshall Tayse and I, Tessy McGuigan, fly over this amazing country of Canada on our way to Ireland. I feel this will be a journey of many discoveries, one that will include as many questions as it does answers. I know when I step on to that sacred ground, the legacies of my ancestors will fill my soul. I ask the Lord and Lady to watch over us and guide me to whatever path leads towards the greater good of the hereafter. This is a journey my mother and the gifted Haggertys before us may have started, but I am to finish.

She tucked her journal back into her bag and retrieved the amulet. She dropped it into her hand out of a lovely velvet pouch she had since transferred it to. She spent the next few minutes deep in thought with it. She stroked it and turned it over and over again, wondering where this mysterious trinket would lead her. What adventurous journey was she bound for? She dropped it in the pouch and carefully tucked it back into her bag. She laid her head on Marshall's broad shoulder and drifted off to a time of deep forests, castle towers and lush, misty moors.

Recipes

Divine Healing Salve

¼ cup (50 ml) sweet almond oil

3 tbsp (45 ml) coconut oil

2 tbsp (30 ml) beeswax

¼ cup (50 ml) aloe vera

¼ cup (50 ml) calendula tea

1 tbsp (15 ml) vegetable glycerin

¼ tsp (1 ml) sodium borate

15 drops calendula infused oil

20 drops lavender essential oil

8 drops tea tree essential oil

In double boiler or a glass bowl set over a saucepan of water combine and heat the almond oil, coconut oil and beeswax until melted. In a separate pot heat aloe vera, tea, vegetable glycerin and stir in sodium borate. Once heated and the sodium borate is well dissolved, remove from heat and set aside to slightly cool.

Pour oil mixture into blender or bowl and let cool for 5-10 minutes (until oil mixture starts to cloud). Start to blend and slowly add the aloe vera mixture. Blend 15 seconds then add the calendula oil and essential oils. Blend for an additional 25 seconds or until well mixed. Pour into containers, let cool and cap.

Exotic Encounters Perfume

2 tsp (10 ml) sweet almond oil or jojoba oil

25 drops patchouli essential oil

15 drops frankincense essential oil

10 drops of neroli essential oil

Fill a small bottle ½ full with sweet almond oil. Add the essentials oils, place cap on bottle, shake, then pour in remaining almond oil, shake again.

Fresh Start Cookies

¾ cup (175 ml) butter / margarine

¾ cup (175 ml) brown sugar

1 egg

½ tsp (2 ml) vanilla

¼ cup (50 ml) unsweetened applesauce

1 cup (250 ml) all-purpose flour

¼ cup (50 ml) whole wheat flour

1½ cups (375 ml) quick rolled oats

½ tsp (2 ml) baking soda

½ cup (125 ml) sunflower seeds

½ cup (125 ml) dried apricot finely chopped (or dried fruit of choice)

1 tsp (5 ml) cinnamon

¼ tsp (1 ml) nutmeg (ground)

¼ tsp (1 ml) cloves (ground)

½ tsp (2 ml) dried rose petals (ground) (optional)

In a large mixing bowl cream together softened butter and brown sugar. Add egg and vanilla. Beat until smooth, then mix in applesauce. In a separate, bowl combine all-purpose flour, whole-wheat flour, rolled oats, baking soda, sunflower seeds, spices and rose petals. Slowly add dry ingredients to the butter mixture. Then add the apricots and blend well. Drop onto cookie sheet 2" apart and bake at 375 degrees for 8 to 10 minutes or until lightly browned.

Heavenly Milk Bath Salts

1 (250 ml) cup Epsom salts

½ cup (125 ml) powdered milk

2 tbsp (25 ml) baking soda

10 drops lavender essential oil

10 drops patchouli essential oil

5 drops geranium essential oil

Mix well in large bowl and let stand overnight to blend. Transfer to airtight container or containers. Add ½ cup to bath and swish with your hand while water is running. Climb in, sit back and enjoy!

Leprechaun's Limelight

1 frozen limeade concentrate

½ cup (125 ml) water

2 liter bottle tonic water or soda water

1 tbsp lime cordial (2 tbsp for sweeter)

ice

lime slices

Combine the limeade, water and cordial in pitcher and stir until well blended. Pour in tonic water right before serving. Add ice and lime slices. Note: Tonic water will make your beverage glow, especially under black lights! Great for Halloween, as well!

Magical Cleansings

1 bucket full of warm water

½ cup (125 ml) vinegar

10–25 drops (total) of essential oil of choice or combination of (see The List)

Misbehaving Tea

1 tsp (5 ml) raspberry leaves

1 tsp (5 ml) red clover

1 tsp (5 ml) black currants

1 pinch lavender buds

Pour boiling water over the tea mix. Steep in teapot for 5–10 minutes. Add honey or pinch of Stevia to taste.

New Beginnings Tea

2 heaping tbsp (30 ml) raspberry leaves (dried)

2 heaping tbsp (30 ml) nettle leaves (dried)

8 rose hips (dried)

2 tsp (10 ml) melissa (dried)

Pour boiling water over the tea mix. Steep in teapot for 5-10 minutes. Add honey or pinch of Stevia to taste.

Sore Joint Balm

½ cup (250 ml) coconut oil

3 tbsp (45 ml) beeswax

2 tbsp (30 ml) castor oil

¼ cup (50 ml) aloe vera

¼ cup (50 ml) strong peppermint tea

1 tbsp (15 ml) vegetable glycerin

¼ tsp (1 ml) sodium borate

10 drops peppermint essential oil

10 drops lavender essential oil

8 drops wintergreen essential oil

In double boiler or a glass bowl set over a saucepan of water combine and heat the coconut oil, beeswax and castor oil until melted. In separate pot heat aloe vera, tea, vegetable glycerin and stir in sodium borate. Once heated and the sodium borate is well dissolved, remove from heat and set aside to slightly cool. Pour oil mixture into blender or bowl and let cool for 5-10 minutes (until oil mixture starts to cloud). Start to blend and slowly add the aloe vera mixture. Blend 15 seconds then add the essential oils. Blend for an additional 25 seconds or until well mixed. Pour into containers, let cool and cap.

Caution: Do not use during pregnancy. Exercise great caution when using wintergreen essential oil.

Whoop-Tuddy Tea

2 tsp (10 ml) fennel seed

½ tsp (2 ml) caraway seed

pinch of anise

Place in a mesh ball in a cup and pour boiling water over the mixture. Let steep. Add honey or pinch of Stevia to taste.

The List

of Aromatic Healing and Magical Characteristics Associated with Herbs and Oils

Apple – *love, knowledge, healing*

Anise – *youth, purification, protection*

Apricot – *love*

Basil – *wealth, protection, love, knowledge, relieves fatigue*

Bay – *prosperity, love, protection, healing, clairvoyance, refreshing*

Bergamot – *success, clarity, calms the nerves, uplifting*

Black Currant – *drives out negative influences*

Calendula – *protection, prosperity, comforts children, attracts your soul mate*

Caraway – *health, protection, anti-theft, mental*

Castor – *protection, negativity*

Cedar – *protection, focus, healing, strength, spirituality, money, high vibration, purification, calming, warming*

Chamomile – *peace and harmony, purification, love, healing and protecting children, rest, money, depression, soothing, calming*

Cinnamon – *prosperity, healing, grounding, warming, protection, love, invigorating*

Clary Sage – *balance, wisdom, clarity, uplifting, purification, sensuous*

Clove – *money, protection, warming, energizing*

Coriander – *healing, love, both relaxing and stimulating*

Eucalyptus – *healing, protection, cooling, energizing, purification, refreshing*

Fennel – *healing, protection, purification, courage, revitalizing*

Frankincense – *spirituality, protection, courage, luck, calming, uplifting*

Geranium – *different colour meanings; pink – love; red – protection; white – fertility, balancing, refreshing*

Grapefruit – *attunement, co-operation, cleansing, stimulating*

Jasmine – *wealth, love, self-acceptance, prophetic dreams, euphoric, aphrodisiac*

Lavender – *love, protection, calming, healing, peace, happiness, longevity*

Lemon – *happiness, energizing, longevity, friendship, purification, exams*

Melissa – *comforts the heart, drives away melancholy, success, courage, uplifting*

Neroli – *stress-release, romance, exhaustion, success, uplifting*

Nettle – *healing, protection, lust, grounding, negative emotions*

Nutmeg – *health, luck, fidelity, comforting, elevating, euphoric*

Patchouli – *wealth, fertility, sensual, relaxing, uplifting*

Peppermint – *energizing, healing, purification, clarity, love, restorative*

Pine – *healing, purification, money, fertility, reviving, strengthening*

Raspberry – *protection, love, fertility*

Red Clover – *removes negative spirits, brings good fortune, encourages honesty*

Rose – *love, protection, healing, harmony, luck, uplifting, tender*

Rosemary – *memory, clarity, protection, healing, forgiveness, refreshing, strengthening*

Rose Hips – *encourages romance*

Sage – *wisdom, protection, wishes, longevity, anger*

Sunflower – *confidence, helps you stand out in a crowd*

Tea Tree – *cleansing, healing, strength, penetrating, stimulating*

Thyme – *courage, healing, purification, love, restorative, reviving*

Vanilla – *love, grounding, mind, lust*

Wintergreen – *warmth, protection, healing*

Yarrow – *love, courage, happiness, protection, self-worth*

Acknowledgements

First, thank you to my spirited, talented editor/publisher, Darcy Nybo of Artistic Warrior Publishing. Your expertise, dedication, knowledge, patience, and humour are second to none and greatly appreciated. I am blessed to have you as my publisher and as my friend. I look forward to many more years and books together.

Thank you to the super, talented illustrator, Magdalene Carson, for the stunning book covers she has created for me. As I have mentioned before, anyone who says you can't judge a book by its cover has not met Mag! Also, a big thank you to Angelika Matson for creating my awesome Web page and helping me with my computer woes. You are the whiz kid!

Thank you to my husband, Wayne and our beautiful, blended family. If it weren't for you, the stories of Tessy McGuigan would never have been written. I love you all, Rob (Joanne), Sabrina, Darren (Holly), Chris and our grandchildren, Tarquain, Julianna (Dan), Xavier, Kaswell, Nishea, Harlow, Griffin, Harper, our dear departed Piper and our little boy on the way! Our great granddaughter Adrianna and your little brother also on the way! These books are especially for all of you. A big thank you to Chris and Chelsea for bringing those well travelled newspapers home from Ireland.

Thank you to my sister Diane and brother-in-law Bill for your unwavering love, support and for the proof reading, my brother Craig and sister-in-law Karen for your love and sitting through more than one book reading, sister-in-law Kath for your love and best wishes.

My in-laws, Shar, Ken, Rick, Frankie, Gail, Rocky, Unis and Leona thank you for your love and encouragement. Thank you to my dear friend Monica for proof reading as well as your constant love and for travelling on this journey with me. It's been quite a ride and will continue to be so until the journeys end, I'm sure!

Last, but certainly not least, a huge thank you to all my remaining family, friends, and new acquaintances for the love, support and encouragement you shared with me after reading my first book, *More Than a Wise Woman*. Your kindness inspired me to write this sequel you now hold in your hand. Apparently, Tessy has touched your lives in the same way she has mine and for that I am humbled.

A special thank you to my Facebook friends! Reconnecting has been such a joy. Your support, friendship and daily humour is so enjoyed and has united us in a sisterhood/fellowship that is truly amazing. I wish I could name every one of you but you know who you are!

Blessed Be!

About the the Author

Elaine Gugin Maddex is a wife, mother, grandmother, and author. She was born and raised in the small town of Minnedosa, Manitoba, where as a small child she followed her grandmother about and helped her tend her massive gardens. This left a huge imprint on her life and the small town girl always remained.

Elaine is a kitchen herbalist who enjoys concocting herbal remedies, spending time in her herb and perennial gardens, working on her next book, and enjoying time with family and friends.

Elaine lives on an acreage in Alberta with her husband, two dogs, two cats, and a wide array of wild birds and local critters.